CHAPTER ONE

In the summer of 1869, when I arrived in the Wyoming township of Beecher's Gulch, I was in my thirty-fifth year. I was christened Weston Gray but among the tribes of the Arapaho and Sioux I am known as Medicine Feather. I've lived and travelled with them for twenty years, sharing their summer hunts and their winter deprivations; fighting their enemies and dancing at their ceremonies; speaking as an equal around their village fire, and as their spokesman at treaty meetings with the white man. Among the nomad tribes of the Plains the name Medicine Feather is acknowledged with honour. My own people tread cautiously when they hear the name Wes Gray.

I have been a trapper, a wagon-train scout and, for a short while, during the last weeks of the War between the States, a reluctant army scout. A Confederate sniper put a lump of lead in my right thigh and the war ended before I was fit again for service. Since then I've ranged the land north to south and east to west, spending each winter with Kicking Bear's Arapaho people in the Wind River country. Come spring I take my haul of beaver pelts to Fort Bridger, along the Oregon Trail, and set by enough money to stock me with provisions for the following winter. Then it's east, to Steelsville, a small town east of Council Bluffs, where I wait for word from Caleb Dodge. I'm the chief scout for the wagon trains he leads west. Sometimes we take settlers to the farm lands of Oregon, and sometimes, their minds still lured by thoughts of gold, we take them to California. Now and then we've made the shorter trip to Montana. Virginia City, once a haphazard arrangement of tents and flimsy structures, now boasts those icons of civilization, a church, a school, a hotel and a jail. Settlers, encouraged by the government, are pouring into the area. The land is good for cattle grazing and farming. Only the truculent Sioux are a cause of anxiety.

But this summer I hadn't got my telegraph message from Caleb. He'd been sore at me during our last trail to California. Sore because I'd married Marie Delafleur, the daughter of a French baker, one of the families we'd led to Virginia City when the war still raged in the South. I could accept Caleb's disagreement with my marriage but I couldn't accept that he wouldn't avail himself of my services because of it. We both knew I was the best scout west of the Missouri. Still, that year his wife had taken a sudden fever and died. The fact that he hadn't been with her played on his mind for a while and excited some religion in him that I never suspected existed. I'm not saying he hadn't been a good man before that, but he'd looked at the necessity of things rather than their face value. He hadn't questioned my need for two wives, I didn't understand why a third angered him so. He ranted and swore at me like I was a devil bearing gifts of sin. I suppose it was because my marriage to Marie was preacher-spoke, but that didn't make it any more real than my marriages to Little Feather, the Arapaho who lived in the village on the Snake, and Sky, the Minneconjou Sioux girl who chose me after the death of her first husband.

Let me explain about living in this vast land. There are no rules that guarantee survival. Strangers are regarded with suspicion by white men and red men alike. Actions which threaten the accepted behaviour of a society are punished, usually with pain and death. To be accepted into a strange community means adopting their ways, recognizing their laws, observing their religion. I'd wintered with the Arapaho for several years before I took Little Feather as my wife. Apart from the feeling that Little Feather and I had for each other it was a symbol to the entire village that my relationship with them was permanent; their needs were my needs, their enemies my enemies, their struggles my struggles. From that point on I was one of them, a brother of the Arapaho. Not only did they teach me their spoken tongue, but through them I learned the sign language common to the tribes of all the nations that wandered the Plains.

Sky's first husband had been a white man, a settler who had worked a triangle of land where the Mildwater Creek ran into the Platte. After his death she chose me as her husband. Such is the way of the Sioux. A widow may choose the warrior she wants in her tepee. Again, setting aside our mutual attraction, we each gave the other an insight into an alien way of life, an insight as vital to the survival of the Sioux as a people as to me as an individual. The Sioux were more anxious to understand the ways of the white men than most of us were to understand theirs. Their way of life, their existence, was threatened by the advancement of the white people. They needed someone like me to speak for them. My service to them meant their co-operation with me when I led the wagons through their land. My Sioux wife provided evidence that when I spoke for the Sioux my words were true.

But a Sioux wife may leave her husband and take another without recriminations. If my long absence from Sky's lodge displeased her she was at liberty to choose someone else, and, perhaps one day, I would ride into the village on the North

Platte and find the lance and shield of another brave outside my tepee. I would accept that. A warrior doesn't mourn the loss of parents, children, wives or horses.

Little Feather knew about Sky and Sky knew about Little Feather. Neither objected to the other. I was a warrior who travelled far and they understood a man's needs. I wasn't able to provide for either of them in the traditional way of their people, I was rarely in the villages when the buffalo came, but I brought white man's goods that I shared with her relatives so that my wives were brought meat and hides while I was away.

Marie Delafleur was different. I married her for her survival. Her family had been part of a wagon train who'd made the shorter journey to Montana. Her parents were French immigrants who had arrived as newlyweds in New Orleans, moved to St Louis with two young children and finally headed west to Virginia City to establish a family bakery business. But disaster befell the family. Charles Delafleur was crushed to death while repairing a wagon wheel just two days short of the journey's end. His wife, Elinore, having opened an eating house, less grand than had been her dream but providing meals that ensured a constant line of customers, was shot dead less than six months later. She got in the way of a drunken roustabout's bullet and died instantly. The townspeople hanged him before he'd sobered up.

Marie, with the help of a local widow and her son, kept the business going. Her brother, Giles, a bright lad, she sent back East to college. But Virginia City was no place for a young girl alone. The town was full of ne'er-do-wells; drifters who hadn't settled after the war, riff-raff looking for an opportunity to fill their pockets with other people's money. Their intentions toward Marie were obvious as their eyes followed her every step.

To keep her more lecherous pursuers at arm's length she'd got in the habit of telling them she was my girl. True enough, there'd been some sparking between us on the way to Montana but that was never going to amount to anything because she wanted a man at home in a ranch house or on a farm, and I wasn't ready for that kind of life. I'd promised her family I'd look them up whenever I was in Virginia City, and when I returned it was easy to fall into the way we'd been the previous year. I soon learned of her ruse for keeping away unwanted suitors and I fully approved. Her family had been good to me on the trail and I was happy to give her what protection I could. To give truth to her claims, we married, and if that seems a cold statement let me reassure you that our relationship was quite the opposite. I loved Marie as much as I did Little Feather and Sky, and like Sky, when the time came that someone replaced me in Marie's thoughts, as it surely would, I would ride on. But while she was my wife

I knew that no one in Virginia City would interfere with her. I had Indian ways of killing people that would exact the most dreadful revenge.

When Caleb's telegram didn't arrive by the second week of June I rode south to Independence where he assembled the wagons he would lead west. It didn't take long to discover why I hadn't heard from him. His horse had fallen and rolled on him, breaking his right leg and three ribs. Fears that his lungs had been damaged were now removed but he'd spent a painful and feverish two weeks and was still bedridden. Another leader had been found for the wagons he had proposed to lead to Oregon and there was no job for me.

Caleb looked pale and older when I visited him at his sister's home. We exchanged pleasantries until she tactfully withdrew saying, 'I suppose you men will want to talk!'

'Pleased you came,' said Caleb. Trying to make himself comfortable seemed awkward. He shuffled in the bed, his face showing the discomfort that movement gave him.

'Wondered why you hadn't contacted me.'

'Yeah. Fell under the horse on the way to the telegraph office.'

'Could have told the fellow who'd taken over that I would scout for him,' I said.

'I know. But I didn't want you to do that.' I threw him a questioning look. 'I need a favour, Wes.

Something I was going to ask you to do even if I hadn't had the accident.'

'What is it?'

'I've had a letter from Annie, my niece. Seems that her and her husband have got themselves some trouble.'

'What kind?'

'Can't rightly say, but she sure sounds worried. Now that her parents are dead she doesn't seem to have anyone else to turn to.'

'What did the letter say?'

'Someone's trying to ruin them. Run them off their land. Even poisoned some of their stock.'

'Does she know who's doing it?'

'Didn't mention any names in the letter. Says there's nothing she can prove against anyone.'

'I guess that means she hasn't involved the law.'

He shook his head. 'Damnation,' he said as he tried sit up higher in the bed.

'What do you want me to do?'

'Go out there. See if there's anything you can do to help.'

'Where are they?'

'They've got a spread in Wyoming. Near a place called Beecher's Gulch. Tarnation, I'd go myself if it weren't for this busted leg.'

The wagons had gone without me. There didn't seem much else to do.

After ten days in the saddle I sat on a ridge looking

down on the one street of timber buildings that was Beecher's Gulch. Dust coated my face and clothes, and the tired muscles of Red, my saddle horse, quivered as we paused there. The anticipation of a cold beer in the saloon drew my tongue along my lips. I tapped Red's neck with the knuckles of my right hand, no need to use spurs, and he began to pick his way down the trail to the town. As the full length of the street came into view I could see a cluster of people outside a building three-quarters of the way along. Judging by the number of cow-ponies at the hitching rail out front, it had to be the saloon. Voices, indistinct, a low murmur, came to me as I reached the beginning of the town. Suddenly the crowd began moving, moving like an emptied bucket of water in my direction.

Now the voices were louder, clearer. 'String him up.' 'Get a rope.' 'Tie his hands.' 'Let's get it done. Thief.'

There were about two dozen men, some waving rope lariats, others gesticulating with unholstered handguns. They came forward, the front two dragging between them a young man whose face was bloodied and whose expression showed both anger and fear. He wore a crumpled, plain white shirt over denim work pants. His gunbelt was empty. His head was bare. As they drew level with me he renewed his struggles. Those closest to him punched and kicked him while the men at his sides held his arms. This was a lynch mob. I'd seen them before, surely and swiftly dispensing justice. There was a big tree at the beginning of the street. I'd passed it on my way in. That was where they were heading. The prisoner was trying to talk. I heard him tell them they were making a mistake. I'd heard every lynching victim say the same words. I let them pass. It wasn't my business.

A storekeeper came to his doorway. 'What's happening?' he called.

'Rustling,' someone answered him. 'Caught red-handed.'

'Who is it?'

'Charlie Darke.'

I pulled Red to a halt and turned him back to watch the mob. Charlie Darke was the man I'd come to see. The husband of Caleb's niece.

CHAPTER TWO

They had got their man on a horse and someone had thrown a noose over a high branch of the tree, one man busily securing the loose end of the rope to a lower branch while another, mounted, slipped the noose over Charlie Darke's neck. The rest of the mob stepped aside to leave a clear run for the horse when the preparations were complete. Charlie Darke had run out of words. Only his eyes, wild with fear, appealed to the men around him. Their bravado, too, was on the wane. Fewer people were shouting as the realization of their actions dawned on them. Charlie found some words. 'Please. I didn't do it.'

A big man bustled his way to the horse's rump. His clothes rough and dusty, his wide face unshaven. In his right hand he carried a coiled lariat. 'Let's get it done,' he yelled, and raised the rope to slap the beast's hindquarters.

I'd already drawn my rifle from the saddle boot,

and as his hand raised I took careful aim and fired. His yell and slap on the horse's rump coincided with my bullet splicing the rope where it hung over the branch. The horse, with Charlie still in the saddle, galloped down the street toward me. Someone, perhaps the owner of the horse, stepped into the street to stop its charge. I put a bullet in the dust near his feet to discourage him. Charlie, noose around his neck and hands tied behind his back, galloped past me.

Though my words were hardly necessary, I yelled, 'Keep going.' I swung the rifle round to cover the astonished mob. I began backing Red along the street, steadily pointing the gun at the centre of the mob.

The big man tried to rile the others. 'Don't let him get away with this.' He pointed at me. 'He can't shoot everyone.'

'I'll make sure I shoot you first if anyone tries anything.' No one did, because they knew as well as I did that I was now beyond the range of their handguns. I hadn't seen anyone carrying a rifle. No one was a threat to me while I had them covered.

A shuffling on the boardwalk to my right caught my attention. It was the storekeeper, a slim, greying man, a full-length white overall tied at his waist and a broom in his hand poised in mid stroke. 'I ain't no threat to you,' he said. 'But he might be.' He indicated with his head to the build-

16

ing across the street. The door was beginning to open.

A balding man with a heavy paunch was shielding his eyes against the glare of the sun. He wore a bemused expression as he looked first at me, then at the group at the far end of the street, then back to me. 'What's going on?' His voice didn't carry a great deal of authority and it wasn't clear whom the question was aimed at, but there was a star pinned to his shirt-front. His gun was still in its holster.

'Just stay there, Sheriff,' I told him, 'and there'll be no reason for anyone to get hurt.'

He squinted against the sunlight and examined my face. Red continued to back down the street. When we reached the last building I turned him and put him to the gallop. I heard a couple of shots fired by someone in the mob. A token gesture. The slugs would have dropped in the dust half-way up the street.

I could see Charlie Darke ahead. The horse was running hard, the free end of the rope around Charlie's neck snaked through the air behind him. They were on a trail that led into open grassland. I put my rifle back into its boot and urged Red to greater speed. Within minutes we'd caught them. I grabbed the bridle and brought both horses to a standstill.

Charlie gushed out words of gratitude as I sliced through the rope that bound his hands. 'Thanks, mister,' he said. 'I don't know who you are but I'm sure pleased you turned up when you did.' He removed the noose from about his neck and flung the rope into the long grass.

'Conversation'll keep 'til we get back to your spread. I don't expect the townspeople will ride after us but whoever charged you with cattle rustling may be reluctant to see you get clear away.'

'It ain't true,' he said, 'I didn't steal any cattle.'

'Like I said, this ain't the time or place for conversation. Lead on.'

It took half an hour to reach the small ranch that lay in the lush meadow west of the Powder River. There was a house, a barn with a privy behind, and another building that could have been a bunkhouse for half a dozen men. The house was mainly timber but a stone chimney rose at one end and dull grey smoke drifted from it. There was a veranda on the west-facing front where a woman stood and watched our approach. We came between two corrals, one of which was empty while four placid horses watched us from the other.

The woman stepped down from the veranda as, in a cloud of dust and scattered pebbles, we drew our horses to a halt.

'What's happened?'

Charlie wiped his brow as though confused by his wife's question, then jumped from the saddle to take his wife in his arms.

'Whose horse is that?' she asked. 'Where's your hat? And your gun?'

Charlie held her by her upper arms and looked down into her face. Unable to find any easy answers he said, 'Come inside. I'll tell you what happened.'

Annie Darke was a pretty girl. Her hair was fair and tied back with dark ribbon. She wore a chequered shirt above well-worn, dusty blue pants. Her figure was good, her body looked strong and the set of her mouth showed determination. An ideal frontier wife. She turned her head and caught me studying her. I removed my hat and flapped it against my leg to remove the trail dust. Charlie suddenly remembered I was there.

'Oh, this is eh. . . .'

'My name's Wes Gray, Mrs Darke.'

They spoke together. She said, 'Wes Gray? I know that name.' He said, 'How did you know my name was Darke?'

'I heard your name in Beecher's Gulch,' I told him, 'and perhaps, Mrs Darke, your uncle has mentioned me. That's why I'm here. In response to the letter you sent your uncle, Caleb Dodge.'

'Uncle Caleb sent you?' There was a note of hope in her voice that hadn't been there before.

I explained about his injuries and got them to tell me about the incidents mentioned in the letter. Annie Darke told me the story.

'After the accident that killed Ma and Pa nothing's gone right.'

'Tell me about the accident.'

'Their buckboard overturned on the way home from church. They were found at the bottom of Congress Ridge by some of the Silver Star riders.'

'The Silver Star?'

'That's the biggest spread around these parts. Duke Barton is the owner. His word is all but law with the other ranchers and people of Beecher's Gulch.'

'A powerful man.'

'A good man. Fair-minded. He was one of the first to settle around here. People trust him and look to him for guidance.'

'And if people don't agree with him?'

She shook her head. 'Can't think of anything that hasn't been resolved sensibly.'

'Did your parents have any dispute with him?'

'No. The two families were neighbours and friends.'

'Were?'

'Duke and his sons don't visit much since the accident.' A look passed between Annie and Charlie which told me there was more to the story than she was telling. For the moment I let it pass.

'How many sons does he have?'

'Two. Chet and Wade.'

'They both work on their father's ranch?'

'Of course. They've got big herds on a whole lot of land. It takes them and a fair number of hands to run the place.'

'How many hands do you have?' I asked.

'Six, at present. We take on more when we're driving cattle to the depot.'

'They all out herding?'

'They are. Two of them stay out in a line cabin overnight. The others will be back before sundown.'

I went to the window and pushed aside the light-yellow curtain that hung there. I looked to the ridge Charlie and I had crossed to make sure that no one was making their way to the ranch. 'Tell me what's been happening.'

Annie caught a loose strand of hair and tried to fix it behind her ear. She looked directly at me, weighing up, I think, my probable reaction to what she had to say. 'Five weeks after the death of my parents, Charlie and I got married.' I had wrongly supposed them married at the time of the accident. My surprise must have somehow conveyed itself to Annie, but she misunderstood its cause. 'I couldn't run the ranch on my own. Besides . . .' She let the sentence finish itself. 'We had a party in town to celebrate. When we returned that night our barn had been destroyed. A fire. We lost the winter feed and our mare who was in foal.'

'You think it was started deliberately?'

'How else?' Charlie asked.

'Do you suspect anyone?'

'Most people were at the party,' said Annie.

'Most, but not everyone.'

'No. Not everyone. But that's not really signifi-cant. We came back in the buckboard. Someone could have ridden here more quickly.'

'Was the barn still ablaze when you got here?'

'No.'

'Still smouldering?'

'No.'

'Then it had to be someone who left the party early, or who wasn't there at all.'

'Or perhaps Indians,' observed Charlie.

'Did you lose any stock?'

'No. The other horses were still in the corral.'

'Then it wasn't Indians. What reason would they have to fire your barn?'

Annie didn't answer. Kept her eyes lowered to her hands resting on the table.

My next question seemed a foolish one to ask a gal as young and pretty as Annie Darke, but it had to be asked. 'Do either of you have enemies?'

'The Bartons,' said Charlie Darke.

'Charlie!' Annie's voice held an edge of desper-ation, not wanting to accept what was possibly true.

I looked directly at Charlie to encourage him to tell me what they were hiding.

'Chet Barton wanted to marry Annie. She chose me and he can't accept it.'

'Charlie, please.'

'Is this true, Annie?'

'It's true that Chet and I were close friends. He wouldn't do anything to hurt me.'

I asked, 'Was he at the wedding party?'

'He wasn't around at the time. He'd gone east with his father.'

'Did the sheriff investigate?'

'Out of his jurisdiction,' explained Charlie, 'though I doubt if he'd question a Barton at any time.'

'That's not fair, Charlie. Dan Bayles does a good job.' If Dan Bayles was the man I'd seen coming out of the sheriff's office earlier, then I wasn't sure I could agree with Annie. Any sheriff who permitted a lynch mob in his town wouldn't get my vote at re-election time.

Charlie seemed to read my mind. 'It would be interesting to know where he was when they tried to hang me this afternoon.'

Annie lifted her gaze to his face, a look of terror frozen on her own. 'What do you mean?'

'I mean someone trumped up a charge of cattle rustling against me. I was in the saloon, playing cards with that man Butler and Harthope, the undertaker, when that new top hand of Barton's came in with a couple of Silver Star riders. Accused me of overbranding some of Herman Lowe's steers with our Circle D mark. Said I'd chased them across the boundary creek and overstamped the Circle L sign with my own.' Annie's hands flew to her mouth, her eyes wide with disbelief. 'Got the people all worked up and dragged me out to be lynched. I tried to tell them there were people who could vouch for where I'd been all day, that I'd been nowhere near the boundary line, but they wouldn't listen. If Wes hadn't happened along you'd be a widow woman now.'

Her eyes turned to me for confirmation. I didn't think this was the moment to tell her that had I not heard the name *Charlie Darke* I'd have ridden by without giving the matter another thought. Another recipe for survival: Don't poke your nose in other people's business.

'Silver Star riders again,' said Charlie. 'It ain't coincidence.'

Annie Darke looked confused by the whole affair. 'Who would believe you would steal cattle?'

'It was a lynch mob,' said Charlie. 'That's what they wanted to believe. Once the cry of "hang him" went up nobody was prepared to listen to explanations or consider justice. The Silver Star is determined to kill me or drive us out and they don't care how it's done.'

'And this is on account of you marrying Annie?' I'd heard of feuds between men who chased the same girl but they mostly petered out when the girl in question made a decision. Trying to get their competitor lynched seemed to me to be the

24

extreme end of jealousy.

Charlie shuffled across to the window. 'The Bartons had an earlier grievance,' he said. 'I killed their top hand. A man called Straker. It was a fair fight but they don't see it that way.'

'Why'd you fight with Straker?'

'He lost some money playing poker. Accused me of cheating.'

'In the saloon?'

'Yeah.'

'Must have been other people around to see that it was a fair fight.'

'The sheriff stopped us fighting in the saloon. Straker caught up with me later. At the livery stable, when no one else was around. He wasn't as fast with a gun as he thought he was.'

'And you think the Silver Star riders have been after you?'

'I'm new in town. Nobody sides with a stranger.'

'Ma and Pa did,' said Annie.

Charlie smiled at her. 'Yeah. Your ma and pa brought me out here to work for them when every-one else would have stretched my neck from the same tree they tried to hang me from today.'

'That when you two met?' I asked.

'Oh, I'd seen Annie about town a couple of times. Helped her pa load some supplies on his wagon one day. That's why they spoke up for me when everyone was riled up and wanted me out of town.' He turned suddenly and looked out the window. 'Someone coming,' he said. 'Riding hard.'

'How many?'

'One,' he said.

'You stay here,' I told them. 'I'll handle it.'

CHAPTER THREE

I cradled my rifle in the crook of my left arm and opened the door. The rider was almost at the house, his horse sliding to a halt in an untidy slither of dirt. From behind my right shoulder I heard Annie's voice. 'It's Chet. Chet Barton.' I looked back at her. Her expression had altered. The strain of reliving past events had lifted from her face. Her eyes were brighter, as though she was receiving a visit from a long absent friend.

'Stay here,' I said and went outside.

Apart from eyes that were as blue as a summer sky and which were not subdued even in the shade cast by his wide-brimmed hat, there was nothing remarkable about Chet Barton. His features and his frame were youthful, his hair was an undistinguished brown and his skin was a lighter shade than is normal for a working cowboy. His horse snorted and stamped after its exertions. Chet seemed prepared to step down from the saddle when I got out on to the veranda.

'Don't get down,' I said.

He lifted his head and looked at me. 'You must be the *hombre* who got Darke out of town.' He paused as though expecting some words from me. I said nothing. Eventually he spoke. 'I'm Chet Barton.'

'I know.'

'Come to warn Darke and Annie that a posse is on the way.' He looked back over his shoulder. 'I was on the ridge back there when I saw them. They're only minutes behind.'

'What's it to you, Barton?' Charlie Darke, rifle in hand, stood in the doorway.

'The happenings in town today, I want you to know that that was none of my doing. I didn't know about the double branding and I didn't send the Silver Star men after you. I was on my way here to tell you that when I saw the posse's dust cloud. If you take my advice you'll get out now.'

'Yeah, sure. Take your advice and desert our home so that the Silver Star can grab our land for themselves.'

Chet Barton's lips set in a firm hard line. There was a long pause before he spoke again. 'I don't like you, Charlie Darke. I've got reason not to like you, but even if the business with Annie didn't lie between us I want you to know that I still wouldn't like you. I don't care what happens to you, but I wouldn't like to see Annie injured, or have her see them take you and hang you on your own property. I suggest you ride off until the whole business dies down.'

His words sounded honest enough to me but before I could decide whether, as Charlie had declared, it was nothing more than a bluff to get the Darkes off their land, Chet suddenly jerked upright, his back arching, then he fell from his horse. At the same time I heard the report from a rifle drifting to me from the direction of the ridge. I looked up quickly and saw the tell-tale wisp of smoke that pinpointed the shooter's location.

'Charlie,' I yelled, 'come and help me.' I got to Chet Barton by using his horse as cover. He was face down on the ground. A blood patch, spreading rapidly, stained the left shoulder of his plain shirt. He was motionless and as I lifted his head I feared he was dead. The shooter put a couple of shots near the horse's feet, hoping to encourage it to move away from the house. It danced about but remained loyal to its master, not straying more than a few feet from where he lay, denying the rifleman on the ridge a clear shot at me. I looked around for Charlie Darke. He'd gone back inside. I yelled his name again. The answer was a series of rifle shots from the front window and some shouted advice for me to get back to the house while he kept the shooter on the ridge occupied.

It seemed he expected me to leave Chet Barton where he lay, and, if he were dead, there was little reason why I shouldn't, but I'd felt a fluttering of breath on my hand when I'd lifted his head, so deserting him was out of the question. The only thing I could do was to hoist the unconscious body on to my shoulder and make a run for the house. Charlie had left the door open, one obstacle less for me to worry about.

'Keep firing,' I called, 'I'm coming in.' It wasn't easy. Chet was a dead weight, and I could no longer keep his skittish horse between me and the ridge. Under cover of a sustained volley from the house – and I realized that Annie, too, was using a rifle – I lifted Chet, picked up my own rifle and ran for the open door. It wasn't until I set foot on the veranda that answering shots sang past my head, two of them, both tearing splinters from the door-frame as I passed. Then I was inside. I kicked the door closed behind me. Annie came away from the window and opened an inner door that led to a back room. There was a bed there that I laid Chet Barton on. Annie looked at him and then at me.

'I think he's still alive,' I said, 'but he needs a doctor if he's going to pull through.'

'What can I do for him?' Annie asked.

'Nothing for the moment. We've got our own lives to preserve first.' I told her to barricade the doors and keep clear of the windows.

For the moment the guns were silent. I asked Charlie what was happening.

'Perhaps I hit him,' he said.

'Was there only one shooter?'

'Couldn't say. Just a minute, here they come.' I joined him at the window. There was a bunch, perhaps fifteen men, riding down the trail towards the house. Charlie fired two rounds at them and they scattered, jumping from their horses and finding cover among the rocks and boulders beyond the fence line. I'd rather he'd held his fire. If the posse was legitimate, if the sheriff led them, there was a chance for talking, a chance for Charlie to declare his innocence of cattle rustling. In a siege situation we had no hope of winning. As if to emphasize my thoughts a volley of rifle fire struck the house. Windows broke, wooden frames splintered and lead ricocheted around the room. A small sob escaped from Annie. I signalled to her to lie on the floor.

Charlie acted as though he was unaware of her presence. He poked his rifle out the shattered window and pulled the trigger a couple of times, not firing at any specific target, just being defiant. The glint in his eyes told me that he was as frightened as Annie.

'Charlie,' I said. 'Think what you're doing. You've got your wife here. She may get hurt.'

'What do you suggest,' he answered, 'that I just open the door and walk out there. If they don't shoot me they'll hang me.'

'If the sheriff is out there he'll listen to your story. He's a fair man, isn't he?'

'My wife believes he's a fair man but that was

when her family and the Barton family saw eye to
eye. It's different now. You'll see. They'll hang me
as a common cattle-thief.'

'You can't fight them,' I said, and again, as
though they were being marshalled in military
manner, a fusillade of rifle fire hummed and clattered around the window above our heads.

When the noise of gunfire died away we heard a
voice calling from the yard.

'This is Sheriff Bayles. I'm here to arrest you,
Charlie Darke, and I ain't going away until I've got
you. You can't outshoot us so you might as well give
yourself up now. You've got my word there won't
be any lynching. I'll see that you get a fair trial.
Come out with your hands up, Charlie and no one
will get hurt.'

Charlie's response would have been to shoot at
the sheriff but I recognized the tension in his
shoulders as he began to bring his gun into line
with the window. 'Don't be a fool,' I said.

Outside, Sheriff Bayles shouted. 'You've got
your wife to think about, Charlie. I'm sure you
don't want Annie hurt in a crossfire. I'll give you a
minute to decide.'

'Listen to him,' I urged. 'He's talking sense.'

'Sure. It's sense for you. But it's my neck that'll
be in the noose.'

'Look at the logic of the situation,' I said. 'You
won't clear your name by trying to outshoot the
sheriff. Killing him would only make you a more

wanted man. You'd never be able to live here. If you can prove you weren't involved in overbranding those steers then put yourself in the sheriff's hands.'

His frame relaxed and for a moment I thought it was all over. He stood up and presented himself at the window. 'Sheriff,' he called, 'I'm telling you I didn't have any hand in trying to steal any cattle.'

Sheriff Bayles's words came back low and slow from across the yard. 'That may be so, Charlie, but are you going to deny you've killed Chet Barton. His horse is still here and there's blood on his saddle.'

The look from Charlie Darke told me that his actions were justified by the sheriff's words. 'The people of Beecher's Gulch have been against me since the day I arrived,' he yelled, 'and you all being Barton's men will see to it that I'm guilty for Chet's death no matter what the truth is.' He fired his rifle and I heard a yell from the yard. It didn't sound as though the sheriff had been hit, just forced into scuttling for cover. One or two shots struck the building, then all went quiet. I figured they would be making plans to flush us out. They were sufficient in number to surround the house so all hope of escape was gone. How long they would wait before attacking was debatable but, if I was the sheriff, I would want the action over before dark.

'You seem determined to get us killed,' I said.

'Why didn't you tell the sheriff that Chet is still alive. If they get a doctor to him he'll be able to tell them that we didn't shoot him.'

'You don't get it, do you? They won't be satisfied until I'm dead. I've got what the Bartons want. That's not allowed so I have to be removed. And,' he said as he drew his Colt from its holster, 'if I'm going to pay for Chet Barton's death then I may as well be guilty of it.' He crossed to the room where the unconscious form lay sprawled on the bed. Annie shouted as she realized his intention and ran into the room where Chet lay. I flung myself forward and grabbed Charlie's gun arm. He swung a punch at me with his left hand. It caught me high on the temple and carried more weight than I expected. I staggered but kept a tight hold on his arm, twisting it up so that it wasn't possible to get a shot at Chet. He tried another blow with his left hand but I was ready for it and blocked it before it was half-way delivered. I wrapped my left leg behind his right and forced him backwards over it. We crashed to the floor, me on top, forcing his right arm above his head, hoping, if the gun went off during our struggle, that Annie wasn't in the line of fire. Charlie brought his knee up, aiming at my groin, but, rolling around on the floor as we were, it was a movement lacking both accuracy and venom.

I needn't have worried about Annie. She it was who brought about the end of the struggle. While we grappled for possession of the gun Annie seized Charlie's rifle and with one swift blow, rammed the butt down on Charlie's wrist causing him to release his grip on the Colt. This second-front attack enabled me to swing my right arm in long arc. My fist collided with Charlie's jaw and he went slack beneath me. I dragged him back into the front room and propped him against the wall while I took a glimpse through the broken window.

It seemed the ruckus in the house had attracted the attention of the posse. Men were gazing inquisitively at the bullet-scarred building, their heads clear targets above the boulders they had used as cover. I could see Sheriff Bayles directing men around the rear of the house. A couple of others were cautiously edging forward, seeking closer cover.

'I'm going to call them in,' I told Annie. 'We don't have another option.'

She looked back at Chet's near lifeless body, then down at her husband who was beginning to shake the wooziness from his head. 'OK,' she said.

'Sheriff!'

Dan Bayles answered. 'What is it?'

'Are you still offering a fair trial?'

'You got it.'

'Then the fight's over. Don't come in shooting. There's a woman and a wounded man in here.'

'Drop your guns out the window then come to the door with your hands in the air.'

I did what he told me with my guns and Charlie's. Charlie glowered not just at me but at Annie, too. 'We didn't shoot Chet,' I said. 'There are three of us to tell what happened. It'll be OK.' He didn't believe me but didn't waste his breath with an argument.

Sheriff Bayles and the posse crowded into the house. They bore with them the scent of bravado, proud of their success, peaceful men whose unity had upheld the law. They gathered around us, rifles thrust forward, anxious to shoot us if we showed any reluctance to follow their orders.

'Where's Chet?' asked Dan Bayles.

'Back room,' I told him.

At the sheriff's bidding two men went through to the bedroom. I heard one of them shout. 'He's been shot in the back, Sheriff. The cowards shot Chet in the back.'

My protest that we hadn't shot him went unheeded. Angry voices called us bushwhackers and cattle-thieves. The mood was turning from pride in their work to outrage at our perceived deeds. One of the men who had been in the bedroom bustled his way to my side. He was a big man, unshaven and dusty. I recognized him as the man who had laid his lariat on the horse's rump to hang Charlie Darke.

'Hang 'em here, Sheriff. They've murdered Chet because he was man enough to face them on his own. When he accused them of stealing cattle they shot him in the back.'

'That's not true.' Annie's voice quivered, a mixture of fear and indignation. 'Charlie didn't shoot Chet.' But her voice was drowned by a series of accusations and threats.

'String 'em up,' the big man shouted, and his words were echoed by others in the group.

'You promised us a trial,' I reminded the sheriff.

'And you'll get it. There'll be no lynching while I'm sheriff.'

'We don't need a trial. We know they're guilty.' This sentiment was met with a roar of approval and other suggestions. 'Take them to the barn.' 'There's a good tree by the fence.' 'Fetch a rope.'

Sheriff Bayles's demands were being ignored. Charlie Darke, who hadn't spoken a word since I'd knocked him out, seemed reconciled to his fate, as though being right in his judgement of the posse's behaviour was an occasion of justifiable pride. Annie was crying, pleading for common sense of anyone who would listen. Then amid the mayhem a gunshot brought silence to the crowd.

As the smoke and reverberations died away, I saw a thickset man in the doorway. His face was swarthy and he wore a short, neat moustache. His eyes were dark and deep under heavy lids. The skin was loose about his jaw and neck, as though he had recently lost a lot of weight, but his expression was stern, and, when he spoke, his low voice carried authority.

Duke Barton said, 'Where's my son.'

CHAPTER FOUR

The men separated to allow Duke Barton to pass through to the bedroom. Sheriff Bayles went with him. They were followed by a man of indeterminate age who had arrived with the rancher. He was three inches short of my height, dressed like a cowboy and wearing a wide-brimmed, high-crowned hat. A plait of braided hair hung over each shoulder, and, set deep in the weathered, expressionless face, brown eyes reflected a mind full of knowledge and secrets. He was full-blood Cheyenne and moved with the careful, silent tread inherent in all the tribes of the Plains.

The men of the posse kept their guns pointed at me and Charlie Darke. There was a new air of expectation in the room, a feeling that, after seeing the bullet hole in his son's back, Duke Barton would authorize our lynching and the matter would be closed. The voices from the bedroom were low and the words didn't carry, but the rancher didn't stay there long.

'Arnie,' he said to one of the men guarding us, 'ride over to Blackwater and get Doc Cartwright here urgently. Chet's in a bad way. It'll take a good man to save him now.' The man called Arnie touched his hat and lit out without a word.

'Mr Barton,' said Annie, 'Charlie didn't shoot Chet. Nor did Mr Gray. Don't let them hang them. Please.'

Duke Barton looked around at the assembled men. 'Put your guns up, boys. I know these men didn't shoot my son. He was shot from the ridge, away off the trail. Hawk here,' he indicated the Cheyenne who stood behind his right shoulder, 'saw the whole thing.' He turned to me, studied my buckskin leggings and jacket as though they were as out of place as a Confederate uniform at Lincoln's funeral. 'Hawk tells me you risked your life to save my son. I thank you for what you did.' He held out his hand and I took it. 'I'm in your debt, Mr. . . ?'

'Gray. Wes Gray.'

A murmur arose from several of the men. Duke Barton spoke. 'Seems I've heard the name before. You the mountain man? The companion of Jim Bridger?'

'That's me.'

'Your reputation is known, hereabouts. May I ask what you're doing here?'

'Just visiting. Mrs Darke's uncle is a friend of mine.'

'That the reason you saved Charlie from hanging in town?'

'Uh-huh. Seems the folks have taken a dislike to Charlie Darke. But they're trying to hang him for things he didn't do. He wasn't anywhere near that creek where the beeves were overbranded. If the sheriff checks with the men Charlie was gambling with earlier they'll tell him that he couldn't have been out there this morning. But the sheriff seemed to be keeping out the way when the mob was seeking blood.'

'Now just a minute,' interrupted Sheriff Bayles, angry at my implication, 'I've never let mob rule take over in any town before and I ain't starting now.'

'OK, Dan,' said Barton, 'take it easy. Mr Gray,' he said to me, 'we have a good sheriff here in Beecher's Gulch. Don't be too quick to judge other people's actions. Still Dan,' he turned back to the sheriff, 'perhaps you can talk to these witnesses. If they vouch for Charlie then he's off the hook.'

Subdued by Duke Barton's words, Dan Bayles agreed to follow up on Charlie's alibi. 'But you've got to come back to town with me,' he told Charlie. 'You're my prisoner until your name is cleared.'

Charlie protested, vehemently; protested his innocence; protested he had work to do around the ranch; protested against leaving Annie alone with a killer around.

Duke Barton spoke calmly. 'Sheriff's got his job to do. Go with him. If your story works out you'll be home tomorrow. Besides, Chet can't be moved so, with your permission Annie, I'll hang around here until the doctor's taken a look at him. Some of my men can help with the cattle for the next day or two.'

I threw in my two cents' worth, assuring Charlie that I would be staying around for a few more days. Unhappily he went off with the sheriff and the posse. I watched them go, then went into the bedroom where Annie and Duke stood silently at Chet's bedside. There was no sign of Hawk, the Cheyenne cowboy.

'When will the doctor get here?' I asked.

'Could be three hours. It'll be dark before they're half-way here. The trail ain't too good in some places. They won't be able to hurry.'

'The bullet's still in him. It needs to be got out pretty soon. If it poisons his blood he won't survive.'

'You offering to do it?'

I shook my head. 'I've done it before,' I told them, 'but never one in as deep as that one. Reckon he needs a proper doctor. A good doctor.'

'Cartwright's a good doctor,' Duke Barton said. 'He's the best.' I couldn't fault the conviction in the rancher's tone.

Annie was kneeling by the bed, applying a cold

cloth to Chet's brow. Concern for the rancher's son was apparent in the careful manner she tended him. Her eyes watched his face hoping to see some sign of recovery but his eyes remained closed, his body still and only his shallow breathing acknowledged that life remained. Duke Barton rested his hand on Annie's shoulder and gently squeezed. The weakest of smiles passed between them, both trying to convince the other that all would be well, neither of them fooling themselves.

I turned and left the room. Duke Barton followed.

'Why did she do it?' I wasn't sure his question was aimed at me. I looked at him to see if he had more to say. 'Why did she marry Charlie Darke. Look at her in there. That's where she should be. At Chet's side. I can't understand what went wrong.'

I wanted to say that perhaps nothing went wrong, that she just changed her mind, that she saw something more admirable in Charlie than she did in Chet, but this didn't seem to be the time to say things like that, and, besides, I knew squat about the situation. 'Think I'll take a look around,' I said.

'How long do you intend staying, Mr Gray?'

'Until I'm satisfied that Mrs Darke isn't in any danger. Couldn't go back to her uncle otherwise.'

'You going to be meddling in the sheriff's business?'

'Someone shot at me as well as your son. I mean to find out who. If the sheriff finds out before I do that's OK with me, but I'm not too sure how hard the sheriff will be looking.'

'Let me tell you something, Mr Gray, I meant every word when I told you Dan Bayles was a good sheriff. He has upheld the law here for many years and before you go suspecting that we're talking about my laws let me put you straight. Dan Bayles is incorruptible. I suspect the reason you had to stop the lynching of Charlie Darke today was because Dan was unconscious. He has a medical problem. I believe he has confided only in me and Doc Cartwright. He has diabetes, and, from time to time, he passes out. I've known about it for several weeks. He came to me when it first occurred because he wanted me to appoint one of my men sheriff until a new one could be elected. I talked him into going to see Cartwright and between us, me and the doc persuaded him to carry on. I didn't want to see him submit to the condition. Until now he hasn't let anyone down, although lately he has refused to handle disputes outside the town limits. I was surprised to see him here today and I suspect he came to make sure that there wasn't a lynching. Perhaps he'll resign now. I'll be sorry to see him go if he does.'

I had nothing to argue with. The health of the sheriff was a local problem that didn't concern me. With or without his help I intended finding out who had a grudge against Annie and her husband and the place to start was the ridge where the shooter had hidden himself to ambush Chet Barton. I went out to the barn to get Red. I was busy saddling him when a rider came around the far side of the house at the gallop. Duke Barton stepped out on to the porch.

'Where is he?' The newcomer who jumped from his mount's back was an older, rougher version of Chet Barton. I guessed he was the elder brother. His eyes were of the same piercing blue but his skin was deeper coloured and coarsened by a busy outdoor life. The breadth of his shoulders and depth of his chest betokened a strong man.

'Take it easy, Wade,' his father said. 'He's inside.'

'First our top hand and now he's killed my brother. Why ain't he hanging from that tree. I'll kill the sonofabitch.'

Duke grabbed his son's arm. 'Hold it Wade. Charlie Darke didn't shoot Chet, and your brother ain't dead.'

In mid-stride Wade threw his attention at his father. 'Chet's still alive?'

'Only just. No guarantee that he'll stay that way. We're waiting for Doc Cartwright.'

'Word at the ranch was that Chet was dead.' His anger bubbled to the surface again. 'And if Charlie Darke didn't shoot him then who the hell did? He was here when it happened, wasn't he? So who else could have done it?'

'We don't know who did it,' Duke spoke in a level tone, trying hard to subdue his son's temper, 'but the bushwhacker was on that ridge yonder. Hawk saw the whole thing.'

'Hawk! That goddamn redskin. And you believe him! He's probably part of Darke's plot to ruin us.'

'Talk sense, Wade. There isn't a plot to ruin us. And Hawk's loyalty to this family is not in doubt.' A tense, silent moment passed between them. I climbed onto Red and walked him towards the fence gate.

'Wes,' Duke called. I reined in and turned Red towards the veranda where he and his son stood. 'This is my eldest boy, Wade. Wade, this is Wes Gray. He saved your brother's life.'

Wade lifted his eyes to my face. For a moment there was a change in his expression. I wasn't sure whether it was concern or surprise, but it passed as suddenly as it came. 'You the Indian scout?'

'Done some,' I said.

'Heard the name.' He pulled at the front of his hat then walked into the house.

'I'll be back before the doc gets here,' I told Duke Barton, and rode off along the trail.

Sundown was less than an hour away when I left the Darkes' ranch, but I wanted to find the ambusher's position before all light was gone. I stuck to the trail until a cover of trees took me out of sight of the house. I could have made a beeline for the spot I had fixed in my mind when under fire, but I wasn't sure that I wanted Duke Barton or his son to know what I was doing.

I cut off to the left and made my way up the grassy bank to the high line overlooking the ranch house. When I got within the vicinity of the sniper's lair I dismounted. On foot I was more likely to spot any tracks he might have made. Not that I expected to find any, I didn't know from which direction he'd approached his shooting position or had left it, this was merely habit, doing what I could to make myself familiar with the land. Before I'd found the exact location I knew one thing about the shooter; he wasn't a novice with a gun. It required someone with a good eye and a steady hand to make a downhill shot with the necessary accuracy to hit a man from this distance.

As I followed a drop in the land, a movement at the top of the ridge caught my eye. I placed my hand over Red's muzzle to keep him quiet, let go of his lead rein and moved stealthily through the undergrowth to where I'd seen the movement. It was a riderless horse that did nothing more than raise its head as I approached. I checked its flank. It carried a star brand which I had to assume was the mark of Duke Barton's ranch. Someone had the same idea as me about finding a trail. I figured I knew who it was.

I found him in a delve almost directly below

where he'd left his horse. He had his back to me, squatting, examining something he held in his hand. I watched him for a moment, then looked across to the ranch house to confirm that the view coincided with my memory of the shooter's rifle flashes.

He didn't turn round, he just said, 'You are Medicine Feather, brother of the Arapaho.'

'How do you know I'm not the sniper come back to collect those shells you've found?'

He turned then. 'Because you approach like an Arapaho, still clumsy enough to wake sleeping Cheyenne ponies, but not like other white men whose step is heavier than buffalo running from the hunt. Besides,' he added, 'I watched you ride away from that house. I knew you would come here. This is the start of the trail to the man who tried to kill you.'

'Do you know the man?'

'No. I was beyond the house.' He pointed to the wooded slopes west of the ranch. 'When many men came from town Ice Eyes went to protect his woman. Sent me to bring his father. Darke not good man. I watch to make sure Ice Eyes is safe before going to Silver Star.' I understood why Hawk had given Chet the name Ice Eyes. Names are important to all the tribes of the plains and can change with the events in their lives. I was proud of my Arapaho name, Medicine Feather, which I'd earned by stealing the tail-feathers of an eagle to fulfil the medicine dream of a new chief. Chet's name referred to his unusual physical feature. Even in shade his eyes had a unique quality. I had noted it in the short time we'd faced each other before he was shot.

'And you saw the shooting.'

'But not the man. When you were inside house I go.'

'Why didn't you go after the shooter?'

'Too many white men. They wouldn't believe Hawk. Only Barton believe my words.' He pronounced the two syllables of Duke's surname separately, Bar-Ton, as though they were two words.

I knew he was right. The word of a lawman often couldn't deter a lynch mob from its purpose. An Indian had no chance. It may have been a narrow escape from the rope for Charlie and me, but Hawk had probably made the right decision. Still, Hawk's words had thrown up two points of interest. First, that he thought of Annie as Chet's, Ice Eyes', woman, and secondly that he, too, didn't hold Charlie Darke in high regard. I put both of these matters to the back of my mind and held out my hand for the shells that Hawk had collected.

There were six of them. Metal casings for .44 calibre bullets, stamped with the Springfield name around the base. At first glance they were no different to the ammunition that was in my own gunbelt. On closer inspection, however, I saw that each of them had a half-inch scratch, as though they had been scored by something in the breech or the ejection mechanism of the gun. I pointed out the marks to Hawk. He, in turn, showed me where the man had lain, laying his finger on a mark on a rock where he must have rested his gun.

We found some boot-prints and followed them back from the delve to a hollow where a horse had been tethered. Collecting our own horses we followed the tracks off the ridge down to the trail to town. But the rider hadn't gone in that direction. He'd turned towards the ranch and ridden in with the rest of the posse.

CHAPTER FIVE

We were picking our way down to the road to
Beecher's Gulch when I realized that Hawk was no
longer riding at my side. I stopped and looked
back. They were twenty yards behind, horse and
man, motionless in the late red rays of the day.
Hawk seemed smaller, older, as though shrivelling
in the diminishing sunlight. His lank pony waited,
neck outstretched, head almost touching the
ground, in sleepy uninterest of the cause of their
halt. Hawk's gaze was fixed on the eastern sky. I
walked Red back to be beside him.

'What is it, Hawk?'

His low voice carried the conviction of truth.
'The breeze foretells an unhappy song. The sky is
coloured with sorrow. Birds have gone early to
their trees, afraid that something will shame their
sight.'

'Trouble? At the house?'

'Beyond the house. Beyond the river.'

'We have enough problems of our own to worry

over,' I said, 'let's just deal with those.'

'Perhaps this, too, is our problem.' It was a common enough belief among the people of the Plains that any unusual event affected their lives. Nature governed their circle of life, they depended upon the change of seasons, the course of a river and the coming of the buffalo. Erratic behaviour of birds and animals told them when a predator hunted, or when the scent of unnatural death filled the air. But for me, at that moment, the immediate well-being of Annie and Charlie Darke was uppermost in my mind.

We jogged on down to the road and there split company. I headed for town, anxious to see that Sheriff Bayles was as diligent as the boss of the Silver Star outfit would have me believe. Hawk indicated that he was bound for Annie's ranch where Duke Barton awaited the doctor from Blackwater, but when I looked back he hadn't moved, his concentration still focused on the sky beyond the river.

Beecher's Gulch was in the midst of its end-of-day routine when I got there. Although there were still one or two people on the street they were, in the main, heading home from their day's labour or heading for the eating-house which was two buildings past the sheriff's office. Most of the business enterprises had closed, the bank, the barber shop, the telegraph office, but at the far end of the street the man who ran the general store was once more outside with his broom. I wasn't sure how good his business was but I was pretty sure that nothing happened in town that escaped his notice.

The jangling notes from a badly played piano came to me from the building that had no other legend than *SALOON* painted above its batwing doors. It was too early for anyone other than the die-hard drinkers to be inside, but the pianist played to advertise the fact that the bar was open for business. There were a couple of forlorn cowponies tethered to the outside rail, their owners inside washing away the dust they'd eaten all day.

More or less opposite the saloon was a more respectable-looking hotel. It, too, had a public drinking area but for the moment neither music nor lamplight declared it open to customers. I rode past, touched my hat to the man with the broom on the opposite boardwalk and stopped outside the sheriff's office.

Despite Duke Barton's testimony on his behalf, indeed especially if his devotion to duty was unquestionable, I thought that Dan Bayles should quit his post as sheriff of Beecher's Gulch. His movements were sluggish, his reactions slow and I figured his confidence was no higher than a snail's home. I startled him when I opened the door. He turned wide eyes at me from his seat at the desk, and I sensed reaction to reach for his gun though his hand still held on to the stub of pencil he had been using. He was overweight and ill. It showed and he knew it, and it robbed him of the ability to show any authority.

Still, when he recognized me he showed an affability and courtesy that it was hard not to appreciate, though it did cross my mind that his welcome betrayed more than a hint of relief. He poured me some coffee and sat me down as though I'd come a-visiting, like settler families after a Sunday church meeting. He spoke of a mutual friend, a cavalry major stationed at Fort Kearney along the Oregon Trail, who'd told him some exaggerated accounts of my encounters with Indians, gunrunners and badmen from the Missouri to the Rockies and beyond.

When I got the chance I asked him if he still had Charlie in his cells.

'You're the second one to make that enquiry,' he answered.

'Oh!'

'Sure. Wade Barton was here a few minutes ago. His pa is interested in any developments.'

'What did you tell him?'

'That I'd spoken to Andrew Harthope who confirmed he'd been playing cards with Charlie when the accusation was made.'

'Isn't that good enough for you to release Charlie?'

'Not quite. Seems Andy had just joined the game a few minutes before the ruckus begun. Couldn't say how long Charlie had been in town.'

'What about the other fella?'

'Clay Butler ain't hit town yet. I'll speak to him as soon as he does. I left word at the hotel and the saloon that I want to see him.'

'What's your feeling about this, Sheriff? Do you think Charlie's innocent?'

Dan Bayles rubbed his chin. 'Well,' he drawled, 'Andy Harthope said Charlie's surprise when the Silver Star boys came in seemed genuine. He hadn't noticed anything suspicious in Charlie's behaviour before that. But, like I said, Andy and Charlie weren't together long.'

'And the general feeling about town?'

'Charlie ain't the most popular person in the territory. In fact, if he stood for mayor, apart from Annie I can't think of anyone who would vote for him.'

'Could there be another attempt to lynch him?'

'Not while I'm here, and here I'll stay while I've got a prisoner in the cells. Besides, he's got Duke Barton's protection after that attempt to frame him for shooting Chet. No one will go up against Duke's word.'

I took my leave of Dan Bayles and headed across the street to the saloon. I needed a slug of whiskey. In this dusty Wyoming town I didn't expect anything other than some local rot-gut, but right then anything would do. I had reached the middle of the street when the batwing doors clattered open and a figure strode out, untied a horse from the rail and rode west out of town. The light from the saloon had been behind him, making him nothing more than a silhouette in the doorway. He was a big man, and he moved with the sort of swagger and bravado reminiscent of gunmen I'd met all across the West. A walk that dared anyone to step in the way. If he saw me he disregarded me, but I watched until he'd ridden beyond the end of the street, then stepped on to the boardwalk and into the saloon.

The pianist was still rattling on the keys with enough accuracy for me to recognize 'Golden Slipper'. Some of the dozen men inside looked my way as I made my way to the bar. All except one were sitting at tables around the room. The exception was Wade Barton. He leant against the bar, his body turned in my direction.

'Well, well,' he said, 'if it ain't the famous Indian fighter. Or have I got that wrong? Should it be Indian lover?'

I stopped at the bar several feet from him. I hadn't gone in there looking for trouble and I really didn't want to be at odds with anyone in Duke Barton's family. 'Whiskey,' I told the bartender. He looked at Wade Barton before reaching for a glass.

'Don't you know who this is, Clance? Your saloon is honoured by the presence of Wes Gray.' Wade's voice was loud enough for his words to be a general announcement. 'You can serve him. He ain't all Indian.'

Clance, the bartender, produced a bottle and poured a measure into a small glass. The hum of conversation and the music had stopped. I assumed that everyone was looking in my direction but I didn't turn round.

'Didn't shoot my brother in the back either. Well you can tell he's innocent 'cos he's not painted up for war. 'Course his friend, Charlie Darke, doesn't bother with warpaint so his innocence ain't so easy to prove.'

I tasted the whiskey. It was no better than I'd expected but no worse either. 'Your pa's accepted the fact that Charlie Darke didn't shoot Chet and you should too. I came in here to burn a little dust from my throat, not to get into an argument with you or anyone else. When I've drunk this,' I lifted the glass, 'I'm going.'

'No need,' said Wade, 'stay and regale the citizens of Beecher's Gulch with your exploits along the Oregon Trail. It's not every day this fair town is visited by a legend.' He downed the remainder of his drink and, doffing his hat in an exaggerated gesture, left the saloon.

I let Clance refill my glass, not because I'd enjoyed the first drink or was even in need of a second, but because I didn't want to follow hot on the heels of Wade Barton. His anger at his brother's attempted murder had driven reason from his mind. I didn't want to aggravate his feelings and it seemed to me that the best way of not doing so was to avoid him altogether. Taking time over another drink would give him the opportunity to get off the street before I left the saloon to go back to Annie's ranch.

The whiskey had hardly settled in my glass and the pianist hadn't struck more than half a dozen notes before I became aware that I had company at the bar. There were two of them. One either side, each of them breathing extravagantly through his nose and grimacing at the perceived result.

'I'm down wind of a gosh almighty smell,' said the one on my right.

'You can't be,' replied the other. 'I am.'

'Can't be as bad where you're standing,' said the first.

'Tell you what,' said the other, 'let's swap places and compare.'

They crossed behind me, sniffing all the time, intimating that the smells that assailed them were too vile to be endured.

'Perhaps you're right,' said the first. 'Perhaps it is worse here.'

'No,' said the one now on my right, 'this is the worse side.'

All this time I'd remained motionless, leaving my hands flat on the bar. Clance, standing apprehensively across the bar from me, kept his arms at his side. The music had stopped again and the only sound, other than the voices of my two tormentors, was the stomp of boots and the flutter of the doors as people left the saloon. I turned my head to the right. The boy, for he could not have been more than eighteen, gave me a wide grin. His hat was set back on his head showing fair curly hair flopping over his brow. He had a yellow scarf around his neck and his red-chequered shirt was partly covered by a black leather waistcoat. He carried his gun low on his right thigh and his hand rested on its butt.

'Know what,' said the other one, 'I've come across this smell before. Got attacked once by some Injuns. Never known a smell like it. Dirty, dog-eating Injuns.'

I turned my attention to him. He was taller and older than his companion. He didn't smile. His eyes were hard, his face unclean and unshaven. His gun was worn higher, the butt no lower than his waist. I had a feeling they'd been sitting at a table near the door, but I could have been wrong. What I wasn't wrong about was that I'd seen them both earlier that day. The youngest had been up the tree fastening the hanging-rope to a branch, while the other had been the man who'd slipped the noose over Charlie Darke"s head.

'You know something, Clance,' the older one continued, 'I reckon Wade Barton was wrong. You shouldn't be serving this fella. He smells Injun clean through. Strip him naked and you'll find red skin all over.'

The younger one laughed. It was sad to hear because he thought himself invincible, that he and his partner were in control and could never be bested.

'OK,' I said. 'You've had your fun. I didn't come to town to fight anyone. When I've finished my drink I'm going.'

'What d'ya say, Ben,' said the younger of the two, 'we get him to strip off his clothes right now and let us see what colour he is? Is it red or yella?'

I stepped away from the bar, three, four paces so that I had an angle on both of them. 'It would be a mistake to think that,' I said. I kept my gaze on the young fella, staring into his eyes until the grin froze on his face and the tension provoked a slight tremble of his lower lip. I knew they would work together, that one would only draw if the other did. I worked on the weakest hoping he would back down and walk away. There was an instant when I thought he would, but it flashed by and I saw the look in his eyes alter and harden in a heart-beat and his right elbow jerked as he pulled at his weapon.

I drew and shot the older man through the heart and swung to the other, holding back the trigger and fanning the hammer so that two shots thudded into his chest and dropped him on the floor before his gun had come high enough to threaten me. I held my stance, I was in a sort of crouch, my gun hand still extended. Gunsmoke swirled around my head. Out of the corner of my eye I noticed Clance move towards the bar. It was usual for barkeepers to have a loaded shotgun under the counter. I pointed my gun at him.

'It's OK, Clance,' a voice called from the door. 'I saw the whole thing.' It was Dan Bayles, rifle in hand, pushing through the batwings. 'Seems they were determined to die,' he said.

'Do you know them?' I asked.

'Strangers. Been in town a couple of days.'

'Unusual for saddle tramps to become so involved in a town's business.' I told Dan Bayles where I'd seen the two before. He rubbed his chin as though perplexed by current affairs.

'You want to get something to eat?' he asked. 'I was on my way to the eating-house when I saw people leaving this place in a hurry. Figured trouble was brewing so I came to look see.'

'Have you left Charlie alone?'

'No. Got a part-time deputy who relieves me so I can get a meal under my belt and a walk around town to make sure everything's peaceable.'

'I'll have to pass on the meal. I've got to get back to the ranch.'

CHAPTER SIX

There was an air of anxious anticipation about the place as I galloped into the enclosure of Annie's ranch. Dim lights showed through the windows of the house but the bunkhouse was in darkness. The animals in the corral moved slowly and quietly, as though determined not to disturb the silence. Almost before I'd dismounted the house door opened and Duke Barton stepped on to the veranda. His impatient glances, as though expecting to see more than the one rider, told me that all was not well.

'I thought you were the doctor,' he said.

'How is Chet?' I asked.

Duke turned his head to look back inside the house. 'Not good. He needs the doctor. He ought to have been here by now.'

We went inside just as Annie came into the room from the bedroom. 'He's feverish,' she said.

We stood by his bedside. His head was moving from side to side, not in any sort of frenzy, but deliberately, the neck muscles showing the tension in his activity. Sweat ran freely from his forehead and sounds escaped from his mouth, sounds which weren't real words but which seemed to be a determined effort to convey a message. Annie knelt beside him, applying again the cold cloth to his forehead, speaking gentle words over him.

'That bullet has to come out,' I told them.

'Something's wrong,' said Duke. 'Arnie should be back with the doc.'

'I'll ride towards Blackwater,' I said. 'Maybe I can do something to hurry them here.'

Duke gave me directions to the neighbouring town. 'It's east,' he said. 'Cross the river then go into the high ground. Where the trail splits, head north through the canyon. That leads right on into Blackwater.'

I didn't expect to ride that far, but his directive to cross the river jarred in my mind. I thought of Hawk's words, that the warning from the birds could be a problem for us, and for the first time I suspected he was right.

There was no sign of Hawk or his pony around the ranch buildings. I wondered if he'd gone across the river to investigate the omens that had bothered him earlier. As twilight rapidly receded toward darkness the relief of the landscape, the cottonwoods and hillocks, stood out only in silhouette. I could see the trail to the river. Hopes that oncoming riders would make my journey unnecessary were unrealized. Despite the darkness and my unfamiliarity with the trail I kept Red moving at a good pace. We splashed through the river water and began the climb to the high ground. The trail was easy to follow but there were stretches when it became a narrow, crumbling ridge with long, grassy drops to my left. Red and I negotiated them carefully. An accident to either of us wouldn't help the situation.

We were approaching the fork in the trail when Red threw up his head and gave a high whinny. From off to my left a horse answered him. I drew my rifle and rested it across my saddle as I urged Red forward. There were two horses. One, a saddle horse, untethered, came away from the stand of trees where it had been grazing, and snickered again as it caught Red's scent. I grabbed its bridle and stroked its neck. The brand on its rump told me it belonged to a rider from the Silver Star ranch. A rifle was still in its boot. The other horse was close by and coupled to a buggy. I worked the mechanism of my rifle to make sure that a bullet was in the breech as I approached.

The man called Arnie lay dead on the ground, arms and legs outstretched and hole in his forehead just above his nose. His gun remained in his holster. He'd been shot without warning. Ambushed. In the dark it wasn't possible to identify where the murderer had waited, but there were bushes and rocks aplenty that would serve the purpose.

Doc Cartwright, whom I assumed the other man to be, was slumped in the buggy. He, too, had been killed by a head shot. The motive for the killings seemed apparent. Someone didn't want Chet Barton to recover from his wound. This time they couldn't accuse Charlie Darke. He was already in the custody of Dan Bayles.

There wasn't anything I could do for the dead men. I didn't have time to cover them or protect them from curious animals. The horses I tethered to nearby bushes. Their presence would keep away all but the most determined scavengers. I had to get back to the Darkes' ranch as soon as possible. Duke Barton would send someone to collect the bodies.

I gathered up the doc's medical bag from the floor of the buggy and remounted Red. I put him to the gallop, trusting him to be sure-footed as we made our way back. The thought struck me that if shell cases could be found from the bullets that had killed Arnie and Doc Cartwright, and if they, too, had scratches similar to those on the cases that Hawk had found, it would provide conclusive proof that Charlie hadn't shot Chet. I considered asking Hawk to help me look for them in daylight.

Thinking of Hawk reminded me that I'd expected to see him on the trail. I realized I'd been wrong to assume that he had crossed the river. The double killing had to be the event that 'shamed the sight' of the birds. But he hadn't found the bodies. If he'd come this way he certainly would have done so.

I put thoughts of Hawk behind me. The important thing was to get back to help Chet. The only choice now was which of us would try to remove the bullet. I'd brought Doc Cartwright's medical bag in the belief that it would contain a tool more suitable for probing beneath the skin than my hunting-knife. Whichever one of us attempted the operation it had to be recognized for what it was, a last resort.

The river arrived more quickly than I expected and soon I was wrapping the reins around the hitching rail at the ranch. Duke Barton opened the door before I got on to the veranda.

'Where's Cartwright?'

'Dead,' I said. 'And Arnie. Bushwhacked in the high ground, near where the trail splits. How's Chet?'

My news shocked Duke, and it wasn't just because it put his son's life in imminent danger. His face drained of all colour, his eyes expressing bewilderment at the events of the past day. He didn't even attempt to reply to my enquiry. Annie came out of the bedroom, her jaw set tight to hold back the emotion she obviously felt. Strands of hair strayed across her face and her eyes were wide and watery, like someone who has long been deprived of sleep. The sleeves of her shirt were rolled above her elbows and there were water splashes on her jeans from her ministrations to Chet. She looked around the room wordlessly, eventually her gaze falling quizzically on the medical bag I held.

'We'll have to remove the bullet ourselves,' I said.

'Why? Where's the doctor?'

'He can't make it.' I put down the bag and went past her into the bedroom. Chet remained unconscious, his breathing shallow, his skin pallid beneath a coating of feverish sweat. I confess that at that moment I didn't believe we could achieve anything by trying to reach the bullet. It looked a hopeless task.

'Have you done this before?' Annie was at my side. She'd taken hold of my arm with both her hands, a reflex action, one she probably wasn't aware she'd done, just needing something to hold on to.

'I don't want to give you false hope,' I explained. 'It may be too late to help him.'

'But you'll try. Please, please try.' Her last sentence was almost whispered, almost a prayer.

'Yes, Mr Gray,' Duke Barton spoke from the doorway, 'you must try to save him.'

It seemed I'd been elected surgeon. I wasn't sure it was an honour I warranted or wanted. I'd dug slugs out of men who'd been shot in the arm, the leg, the shoulder and the butt. None that were near vital organs and even then they hadn't all survived. This one was in the back, in deep, and it had to be somewhere near the heart. I could kill him myself just probing for the bullet.

I felt Annie's nervous fingers on my arm and remembered when I, too, had been shot and my Sioux brother-in-law, Throws The Dust, had put my life before his reputation. Chet's father and Annie wanted him to have this chance, and, slim as it might be, who was I to deny it.

'We're going to need some hot water,' I said. 'I need to wash and you need to wash Chet and the table in there.'

Duke set to work drawing water from the pump by the horse-trough while Annie lit a fire in the black stove in the corner of the living-room. All my previous attempts at surgery had been performed with nothing more than my hunting-knife, burned clean in a flame then used to probe, force out and cauterize. Now that I had the opportunity I searched through Doc Cartwright's medical bag, selecting every cutting, probing and gripping instrument I thought might be needed. I asked Annie for a dish to put them in and told her to pour boiling water over them when it was ready.

I sliced away Chet's shirt and, with Duke's assistance, turned him so that I could see his back. Blood still ran from the wound, not heavily, but it had been several hours since he was shot so the loss was now substantial. I knew that the open wound needed some sort of treatment to prevent infection but I had no idea what it should be. If he died while I attempted to remove the bullet then at least I'd tried, but I was more concerned about what would happen if I was successful. I could cauterize the incision but I could give no guarantee that the wound inside his body would be clean.

As though my thoughts were on view Duke Barton's words to me were a comfort. 'I know you'll do your best.'

I washed; hands, face and shoulders, needing to refresh myself as much as to clean myself. When I was done I carried Chet across my shoulders from the bedroom to lay him face down across the freshly scrubbed table in the front room. I checked with Annie that she had a quantity of linen at hand. The bleeding concerned me. I hadn't a clue how to stop it. When I picked up the doctor's scalpel Annie stepped closer with a lamp. I saw that her lips were moving, the words were silent but I knew it was prayer. For a brief moment our eyes met. I wanted to give her some encouragement, but there was none to give. Prayer was likely to be as effective as my use of the blade. I stepped forward, took a deep breath and positioned the point of the scalpel just above the wound.

Then the door opened, the night air shifted the flame from the lamp and I looked up from Chet's naked back. The man held his head high, his nose was long and straight and down his cheeks were two yellow lines. Apart from a deerskin loin-cloth and deerskin moccasins he was naked. In his left hand he carried a short stick attached to which were a series of relics, small bones of animals, perhaps humans. In his right he held a long scalping-knife. He was Cheyenne.

CHAPTER SEVEN

He was not alone. At the Cheyenne's left shoulder stood a young girl of his tribe. Like the warrior she held a proud posture. Her hair hung free but kept clear of her face by means of a decorated, rabbit-skin headband. She wore a beaded dress fringed with porcupine quills, and wore moccasins on her feet. She held tight to a buckskin bundle.

Hawk stood behind them, his high hat towering above his two tribespeople. 'I have brought my children to save your child,' he told Duke Barton. 'I read the signs. They spoke of the death of a wise man. It must be your doctor. No longer can he help Ice Eyes. You must trust these. My people. If Ice Eyes can be saved they can do it. Then, while breath remains in our bodies, we will be equal friends.'

For a long moment silence covered the room. Duke seemed stunned by the suggestion that his son's life should be put in the hands of Indians. He looked first at Annie, then at me. I dropped the scalpel back into the bowl. If someone else wanted the responsibility of removing the bullet from Chet that was OK with me. The Cheyenne, like every other Indian nation, had had to learn about treating gunshot wounds the hard way. It was probable that the medical knowledge of these two Indians – calling them his children didn't necessarily mean they were Hawk's offspring – was greater than mine.

But I had misunderstood Duke's silence. He stepped forward and placed a hand on Hawk's shoulder. 'I'd be grateful for Strong Bull's help.' A look passed between them that was beyond my comprehension. It spoke of friendship, or duty, or some bond between them from which the rest of us were excluded. My willingness to hand over the task was obvious; I hoped that my belief that the Cheyenne had a greater chance of success was equally apparent. I stepped aside and took Annie with me.

That Duke had recognized the warrior, knew him by name, made it more likely that Strong Bull was Hawk's son. Strong Bull sang a low song and shook his relic stick over the unconscious body on the table. His eyes looked at the wound and the body and the face. With Hawk's help he turned Chet on to his back and began feeling with his fingertips the area where the bullet would have exited if it had gone clean through. I suggested to Annie that she should get some rest while Strong

Bull and the girl worked on Chet Barton, but she refused.

'You've nursed him for a long time,' I said, 'and tomorrow you'll be needed to do the same again. Go and lie down. If it becomes necessary I'll call you.'

'I wouldn't sleep,' she said. Judging by the wary glances she cast towards the Cheyenne people I knew she didn't share my confidence in their medical abilities. I poured her some coffee from a jug keeping warm on the stove. When I gave it to her a new smell began to permeate the room. I recognized it immediately. The Cheyenne girl had opened her buckskin bundle and spread its contents, several kinds of herbs and berries and bulbs, on the floor. She had selected three or four of them and had begun crushing, chopping and grinding them in an earthenware bowl. They were bound together by the natural juice of the ingredients, boosted by generous portions of her own spittle. The resulting pungent, green paste was a better and less painful way to heal Chet's open wound than my amateur attempts with gunpowder and searing-steel would have been. I'd been treated with something similar myself. Marie Delafleur had been appalled when I refused to replace the long grass leaves that were smeared with the slimy unguent with her store bought ointment, but Sky had mixed and applied the medication and given me strict orders not to remove it for three days. I'd been shot, then tortured by her own people. She'd nursed me back on to my feet. She wasn't going to apply anything to my body that would do me harm. I owed it to her to adhere to her advice.

All this occurred before I was married to either of them. Despite the unpleasant smell and perhaps because of Annie's reaction, I had the comfort of their images in my mind. The tribes had developed their own medical customs and had used them, successfully, for centuries. Annie's face reflected the same abhorrence that such a vile composition should be applied to Chet's body as Marie's had when she found it on mine.

In a low voice, both to give her confidence and to distract her from Strong Bull's scalping-knife which he had laid on Chet's chest, I told her of my own wounds, and of the healing power of the paste the girl had prepared.

By now, Strong Bull had begun to burn some roots. The smoke was thick, dark and foul-smelling. When Annie began to cough I suggested we went outside, but she decided that it would be sensible to rest for a while. She went into the bedroom and closed the door.

I stepped outside. The night air remained warm. I looked up at the moon, a pale shape in the black night sky. From the north, sounds of cattle, uneasy where they lay, carried to me, and all around scents of nature hung in the air. There was a hint of light coming from the bunkhouse. Annie's cowhands had returned, presumably while I'd been looking for Doc Cartwright. There were voices, laughs and shouts, and I guessed they were playing cards with the aid of an overhanging oil-lamp. Perhaps, in the morning, two of them could be persuaded to bring in Doc and Arnie.

Behind me the door opened. With silent step Hawk came and stood with me just off the veranda. He'd discarded his hat, jacket and shirt. He folded his arms across his chest and breathed deeply of the night air. There was something of celebration in his manner, and something of completion.

'When I was a boy there were no white people on this land. The enemies of my people were the Crow and Shoshone. They seldom came this far into our land, but if they did, if they came to steal our ponies, we would fight them and chase them until they returned to their own lodges. Then we would attack their village and steal their women, and later, around the village camp-fires we would tell the tales of our bravery.'

I pretty much knew the lifestyle of the Cheyenne. It didn't differ much from that of the Sioux, Pawnee, Arapaho or Crow. Long ago they banded together to survive and were as likely to trade with other tribes as they were to fight. Battles were usually brief and often bloodless; touching an armed enemy with a coup stick gave a warrior as much honour as killing him. Villages usually consisted of only a handful of families so they needed all their hunters to survive, one death being sufficient to end a skirmish. Then the white men came. At first just another tribe who built permanent settlements, stockades, towns and ranches. But they were a tribe that multiplied, spreading over the land like ice melting in a spring thaw. They wanted and took more and more, pushing the tribesmen towards the hills, away from the buffalo trails and hunting grounds that had long been theirs. And when the white men fought their disregard for the number that died amazed the Cheyenne and Sioux and the other tribes. An Indian village would mourn one dead warrior, the whites, it seemed, merely replaced their dead with another ten, and each one seemed to have only one desire – the death of all the tribespeople.

'When the white man came,' continued Hawk, 'they never had peace in their hearts. They wanted the land we hunted, the rivers we fished and the sacred hills of our ancestors. We lost the fight for our homes. We were forced to follow new trails. It became more difficult to feed and clothe our families. Before he became a warrior, the heart of my son, Strong Bull, filled with a longing to return to the land of his fathers. It was his time for fasting, dreaming his dreams and learning the medicine that would lead his life. Alone, he left the village. His wanderings brought him to the hills above this ranch.' He pointed into the darkness, towards the ridge from which the shootist had fired at me. 'Certain that the spirits had led him to that spot he sat on the ground and sang his dream song. But, though he remained there while the sun blazed and the night chilled his body, and though neither food nor water entered his mouth, no dream came.' I knew what Hawk wanted to tell me: that Strong Bull was confused by his failure to dream. If he'd been led to that spot by the spirits then some vision, hallucination, dream should have taken over his mind. 'He got on his pony to make the journey back to his village. Within two strides the pony slipped and Strong Bull was thrown against some rocks. Bar-Ton found him. When a Cheyenne is found alone and injured by a white man he expects to die. Bar-Ton did not kill my son. He took him to his house. Brought a doctor to heal him. Fed him and looked after him until he was able to travel.'

'That why you hang around here? Repaying Mr Barton for taking care of your son?'

'We do not always understand why the Great Spirit guides us down one trail and not another.' He paused, his stoic features softened by the deep tranquillity in his eyes. He looked into the night as though listening to a secret message that foretold peace for him for ever. 'Strong Bull had his medicine dream in this house. In a fever brought about by his injuries the spirits visited him and told him he would be a great healer for his own people.

When he was able he returned to our village. The value of my son's life to the Cheyenne is high. He fulfils his destiny and heals many people. My value now is small, but I came here because I believed the Great Spirit had need of me here. I thought He wanted me to protect Bar-Ton. Now I know it was just to be a messenger. To bring Strong Bull back here when he was needed. I will stay no longer. When my children return to their village I will go with them. I am pleased my debt has been repaid before it is too late.'

'I think you've been more than a messenger,' I told him. 'Today you've saved my life and Charlie Darke's. Perhaps Annie's, too.' Then I remembered Hawk's words to me when we were examining the tracks on the ridge. 'Why did you tell me that Charlie Darke wasn't a good man?'

'He killed Top Man.'

'You mean Mr Barton's foreman? Straker?'

He nodded. One solemn movement of the head.

'Charlie told me it was self-defence, that Straker had called him out.' I wondered if Straker and Hawk had been friends, but when I asked the question Hawk shook his head.

Before I could question him further we heard the approach of a single rider coming quickly from the south. There was a bustle about the way he rode, arms flapping up and down as though keeping his own body on the move would increase the speed of his mount. He jumped down and strode on to the veranda. Despite the dark I knew it was Wade Barton. Hawk had stepped away from me, moved into the deepest shadows near the door, trying, it seemed, to keep his presence a secret.

Wade Barton lifted his head and looked me in the eye. There was anger in his gaze, worry about his brother, I guessed, but I didn't think that now was the best time for him to be interrupting what was happening inside.

'They're trying to get the bullet out, ' I said. 'Best if you wait here until they're done.'

I couldn't see the expression on his face, the veranda was in darkness and his wide-brimmed hat was low over his eyes, but he stopped and turned to me. 'Cartwright's in there?'

'No,' I said. 'Doc's dead. I found his body and the man called Arnie's up in the high ground where the trail splits north to Blackwater. They were shot from ambush.'

'You found them! How do I know you ain't the one that did the killing?'

I don't take well to accusations like that. My hand moved over the butt of my Colt Peacemaker.

'You killed two men in Beecher's Gulch tonight,' he said.

'And that gives you reason to suppose I killed the doctor?'

'I got no reason to suppose you didn't. You're a

stranger and a troublemaker. Both make you favourite.'

'So guilt and innocence are just based on who you know, are they?'

'Don't know no better rule.'

I was beginning to dislike Wade Barton, but I checked myself, his brother was hurt bad in the room behind me and his pa had saved me from a probable lynching. 'Still best if you wait out here until they're done fixing up Chet.'

'Well if Cartwright ain't here just who is it that's digging the bullet out of my brother's back?'

Hawk emerged from the shadow, but his body seemed so still and erect that there was no suggestion of motion. 'My son. Strong Bull.'

The silence hung heavy. Then a sound reached us from inside the house. It was Strong Bull singing a medicine chant. That was too much for Wade. He drew his revolver and made a lunge for the door. 'No stinkin' Indian's touching my brother.'

I made a grab for his gun arm. He swung it in a vicious arc and though I almost got all the way under it his loaded fist struck me across the top of the head and tumbled me against the veranda rail. I heard him swear at Hawk and threaten to kill him if he tried to bar his way. The blow I'd taken hadn't done any damage and I got back at him, grasping and twisting his wrist so that the gun pointed to the sky. Pivoting on my right foot I smacked my left shoulder into his back with enough force to lift him off his feet. The gun discharged and I flung him off the porch on to the hard earth near where his horse stood. As I jumped on him and aimed a punch at his jaw I was aware of noises from the bunkhouse.

My punch landed on the left side of Wade's jaw and his head banged against the ground. Hawk stepped on his gun hand to eliminate any further risk of being shot while from the veranda Duke Wade's voice cut through the night air.

'What's going on out here?'

'It's your son,' I said. 'He doesn't seem keen on the idea of Strong Bull saving Chet's life.'

'An Indian, Pa. You letting an Indian stick his knife in Chet?'

'He's doing his best to save your brother's life. Same as all these people here.' The cowhands had gathered round us, eager, as ever, to watch a fist-fight. 'If you ain't got the sense to understand that,' continued Duke, 'then git yourself back to our own spread. I'll be home when Chet's out of danger.'

'Or dead,' shouted Wade. He fixed Hawk with a deadly look. 'Chet dies and there's no way you're leaving this valley.' He turned his attention to me. 'And it ain't over between us, either.' His father yelled another warning at him and he climbed on his horse and rode away.

CHAPTER EIGHT

The stench of the medication hit me as soon as I opened the door. Strong Bull sat cross-legged in the far corner and his sister stood beside the table on which Chet was still outstretched. His face was white, as though all the blood had drained from his head, but his chest rose and fell in a strong, steady rhythm. High on the left side of his chest I was surprised to see a dressing which consisted of river-plant leaves smeared with the green unguent that Hawk's daughter had blended. My surprise was due to the fact that the bullet wound was in Chet's back. My expression must have asked the question because the Cheyenne girl picked up something from beside her bundle of herbs and held it in her open palm. It was the small lump of lead that had been inside Chet.

'Pushed it right through him.' There was a note of awe in Duke Barton's voice. 'Strong Bull opened Chet's chest and pushed the bullet out. Must have suspected it was almost through him.'

'He's breathing easier,' I said.

Annie was leaning against the wall near the bedroom door. She looked bemused, holding a bowl in her hands as though unsure what to do with the contents. Her sleeves were rolled up above her elbows and a thick strand of hair hung over her face.

'Let me take that,' I said, crossing to her and taking the bowl from her hands. The water was clean and cold. I put the bowl on the floor and guided Annie outside. The night air was probably all she needed to regain her composure. I walked with her across the compound to the fence line. There was a big tree-stump not far from the gate and that was where she sat, making a beeline for it as though it were the most natural thing in the world. No doubt she'd sat there a lot. We didn't speak. I stood by the fence with my back to her, looking off to the ridge and the trail into town. From time to time I could hear soft sounds coming from her, sobs that she was stifling with her hands. I didn't interfere. Whatever was troubling her would be resolved more quickly without words from me.

Eventually she called me, her voice soft but with a controlled determination. 'Will he make it, Mr Gray?'

'I can't rightly answer that, ma'am, not being a doctor, but what I can tell you is that that Cheyenne in there, Strong Bull, owes his life to

Duke Barton, so if anyone's going to do the best they can to save Chet then I'd say it's him.'

A smile touched Annie's face. Hope brightened her eyes. Then she turned her head away from me, her fingers entwining in her lap. 'I've made a mistake,' she said.

'We've all made mistakes.'

'This is a big one. I don't think I can fix it.' It didn't need a Pinkerton detective to figure out she'd married the wrong man. My attitude to marriage didn't make me the right person to talk to about such matters. If she'd been a Sioux squaw she could have thrown Charlie Darke's belongings out of the house and taken Chet in without anyone batting an eyelid. But she didn't let me off the hook. 'I shouldn't have married Charlie,' she said.

To my way of thinking neither Charlie nor Chet was currently in a position to offer a secure future. What I'd said about Strong Bull doing all he could to save Chet's life was true enough but it wasn't a guarantee of success. Perhaps daylight would give us a better clue as to his chances of survival. And Charlie hadn't returned from town. If his alibi didn't hold water his chances of swinging for cattle rustling were pretty high. Of course these weren't thoughts that Annie wanted to hear. 'Things have a habit of working out,' I said. 'For the moment you've got a ranch to run. Best concentrate on that.'

She looked up at me, her chin tilted in defiant

attitude as though she would bravely do battle with all of life's adversaries. 'If Charlie hasn't returned by daylight I'll go into Beecher's Gulch. Will you come with me, Mr Gray?'

I told her I would. She stood, rested a hand on my arm and gave me one of those quiet smiles that seem to bestow on a man an honour that he knows he doesn't deserve. 'I'm pleased Uncle Caleb sent you,' she said, and headed for the house.

I let her go, unsure of what she thought I'd done for her, unsure what I was going to do myself come daylight. I went back to the veranda, sat in the shadows in the furthest corner from the door and went to sleep.

I awoke to the smell of cooked bacon and hot coffee and the sound of voices, all coming from the bunkhouse. The house was a haven of silence. When I looked in the Cheyenne girl stood near Chet's head, watching him, holding a damp cloth that I think she'd used on his brow. I mixed a few Sioux words in with my hand-signs to find out the condition of the patient. She told me he would live, her voice light, her eyes never lifting to look at my face, her shyness a contradiction to the role she'd undertaken during the night. But Indian maidens were like that, ready to do whatever task needed doing no matter how gory or violent, yet reluctant to look into the eyes of a warrior lest there was an exchange of pleasure in each other's company. Sometimes I wondered how any of them got married, but it was a ritual, their mode of behaviour, they got their message across one way or another. Despite the fact that this girl wouldn't look at me I knew she wasn't afraid of me or reluctant to have me near.

Hawk lay under the window. I thought him asleep but he rose to his feet in a sudden, fluid movement. 'We go now. Strong Bull can do no more,' he said to me.

The girl turned away and left the house, gone to prepare their ponies for the journey back to camp. For a moment I wondered if his abrupt decision was simply a means of separating me from his daughter, but he gestured with his head, wanting to speak to me outside. We wandered over to the tree-stump where, a few hours earlier, I had spoken with Annie.

'Charlie Darke killed Top Man,' he said. 'I saw it.'

'You mean he murdered him?'

Hawk nodded. 'I was in the corral. There were horses for sale. I look at them for Bar-Ton. I heard Top Man in alley. His step I know. Perhaps he looked for me to return to the ranch. Before he reached the stable I heard someone call his name. It was Charlie Darke. He had his gun in his hand. When Top Man turned around Charlie shot him. Then he took Top Man's gun and dropped it near his body.'

'Made it look like they'd both drawn. Why didn't you tell the sheriff?' I knew the answer to that one, so asked, 'Did you tell Duke?'

'Bar-Ton had travelled East with Ice Eyes. They were gone many moons. Other things happened before they returned.'

'What other things?'

'The killing of Annie's people.'

'Her parents?'

Hawk nodded. 'Charlie Darke killed them.'

I was stunned. 'Are you sure?'

'He beat them with his gun then stampeded the horses that pulled their buggy. When it overturned he checked that they were dead then rode away.'

'You saw this?'

'I watched from the high ground. It was done before I could help them.'

'Have you told anyone?'

'Bar-Ton,' he said.

'But nothing's been done.'

He looked past my shoulder toward the house. Strong Bull was jumping on to his pony's back, his sister already sat astride hers and held the lead rein of another. Hawk waited for them. 'My daughter, Calf Woman, travels far to look at you.'

'Me?'

'The stories of Medicine Feather are well known in Cheyenne lodges. But I tell her Arapaho heroes still bleed on Cheyenne lances.' For Hawk that passed as humour. He stepped on to the tree-stump, grabbed a fistful of mane and swung himself on to the spare horse's back. I walked around the horses and stopped beside Calf Woman. Part of my survival policy says don't spurn a possible friend. Who knew when a Cheyenne ally would be needed. I removed my hat and plucked from it the short, white eagle-feather that I keep in the band. I had nothing else to offer. Only the feather. I put it into her hand. Calf Woman hardly raised her eyes from her pony's neck, but she held tightly to the feather. Her father spoke a word, a command, and the three moved forward in stately fashion, like the centre-piece of a royal procession. Before they'd gone six horse-lengths from me Calf Woman turned and smiled. It was the sort of smile that demolished the illusion of shyness that had been prevalent earlier; the sort of smile that made me feel that, in a unique way, I could be the means of uniting all the tribes of the Plains.

Chet Barton's eyes were open when I returned to the house, although they were drained of their colour as his body was drained of strength and his mind, it seemed, drained of awareness. He was looking at Annie, who had taken over Calf Woman's position at the top of the table, but was unable to maintain focus on her when she moved. She was talking to him, gently, insisting that he would soon be back on his feet. She caught me watching her and gave me an uncertain smile.

Duke Barton didn't look a lot better than his son. A near sleepless night had been rougher on him than I'd expected. He was perched on a chair, unsure of his next move. I figured getting him on his feet would bring out the boss in him. The hired hands weren't likely to take orders from me, a stranger, but they'd have some sort of respect for Duke Barton. 'Someone's making breakfast over in the bunkhouse,' I told him. 'Perhaps you can get them to make some for us. And get a couple of the men to cross the river and bring back those bodies from the high country.' It took him a moment to act, but he got unsurely to his feet and went outside.

'Still no sign of Charlie,' I said to Annie. 'When we've had breakfast we'll find someone to stay with Chet then head into town.' She nodded, then, with a critical glance, examined her hands and clothes for the suitability for a ride into town. I left the house and crossed to the water-trough to scoop water over my head and arms. Refreshed and part-ways cleansed, I caught Duke Barton on his way back from the bunkhouse.

'Hawk told me about Charlie Darke,' I said. 'Why didn't you tell the sheriff he'd killed your man Straker and Annie's folk?'

'Wouldn't have done no good. Not a jury in the country that would have convicted him on the word of an Indian. You know that.'

'Could've tried,' I said. 'Besides which Annie

needs to know about the man she married.'

'Yeah. Well, there you got us. Everything seemed set for Annie to marry Chet before him and I had to go East for awhile. When we come back she's married to Darke. Wouldn't have looked good if we'd proclaimed her husband a murderer. People would have said we were riled up because he'd pinched her from Chet. Nobody has any suspicion that her parents' deaths were anything other than accidental.'

'So you were just going to let him get away with it?'

'Difficult to know what to do. Hawk tried to scare him away. Burnt down their barn and procured some poison plants that he fed to a couple of their beeves. I stopped him when I found out about it. Scaring them was just fuelling Darke's reason to sell the ranch.'

'Hawk did those things?'

'You knew about them?'

'They're what got me here.'

'Hawk just thought to scare Charlie away. Didn't think he was the kind to hang around if there was trouble. So we set to watching him, had to in case he tried to harm Annie. He'd have slipped up sometime. We were sure we'd get something on him.'

'Like over branding his neighbour's steers?'

The anger in his retort was genuine. 'That weren't nothing to do with the Silver Star ranch.'

'Perhaps not,' I said, 'but if you've had men watching him then you had to know he didn't do it. But it was Silver Star men who tried to have him lynched.'

'You're wrong. Sure there were some of my men in town when the cry went up but they weren't the ones who started it. Heck, they don't know what he did any more than Dan Bayles does.'

'Still,' I said, 'it would have been a handy way of disposing of him.'

'And it would have saved my boy from taking a bullet in the back.'

'Tell me, apart from you and Hawk, who knows about Charlie Darke?'

'Just my boys. Chet and Wade.'

'What do you plan to do about Charlie now?'

'I don't know.'

I thought a moment. 'Any ideas why he killed Annie's folk?'

'For the ranch'

'He doesn't look like he's done too much wrangling to me,' I said.

'No. But it has another value. A large cash value. There's a valley to the north that has good pasture land with plenty of water for the cattle. The railroad want to buy it. Joe Brookes, Annie's pa, wouldn't sell it despite what was on offer. The alternative for the railroad means bridge-building, blasting through mountains and delays of one kind or another. Some people thought Joe was mad not to

91

take the money but he said the ranch was near worthless without that valley and he didn't want to start settling land again someplace else.'

'The railroad's offer is common knowledge?'

'Sure it is.'

'Is it still on the table.'

'As far as I know. But Annie ain't going to sell up either.'

'How d'you know that?'

A sudden glint of embarrassment reached his eyes. 'Chet and her spoke about it.'

'You mean they talked about what they'd do with the valley if she married Chet.'

'Sure. But it was only talk. Joe and Louisa were still alive. It was still Joe's ranch. But Annie said she was ranching stock and if the ranch was hers she would do exactly the same as her pa.'

'Do you think that's Charlie Darke's plan? Get control of the ranch and sell it off to the railroad?'

'Seems probable, don't it?'

I had to agree it did. Hawk wouldn't lie about Charlie murdering Straker and Joe and Louisa Brookes. He'd killed Straker because he'd accused him of cheating, probably with justification, so the lure of a huge sum of money would certainly make him kill again. I went into the barn to harness up the rig for Annie. I almost hoped that when we got to town Dan Bayles would have found some evidence to prove Charlie Darke's guilt.

CHAPTER NINE

Chet Barton was sleeping when I left the Darke place. Duke had made the necessary arrangements for the recovery of the bodies out towards Blackwater, including, at my suggestion, searching for spent shells at likely ambush locations. Also, he had sent for Annie's neighbour, Mrs Lowe, to come and nurse Chet while the rest of us got on with the things we needed to do. Chet looked weak but there was no fever and he slept peacefully.

Annie, anxious to know what was happening in town, had her bonnet on and was slapping the reins across the rumps of her team while I was still working my way through a platter of eggs and bacon. She was over the ridge and out of sight before I'd drained the coffee from my mug. I'd've appreciated a refill but didn't want her to get too far along the trail without me. I'd promised to go into town with her and I didn't mean to let her down. She'd set her horses off at the gallop, they would soon put distance between themselves and the ranch. I unhitched Red and set off in pursuit.

The trail from the top of the ridge ran straight for half a mile before disappearing through a gap in some low hills. The rig was out of sight by the time I'd gained the high ground, only a hint of dust hanging in the air where it had been. I put Red to a steady gallop. We soon reached the gap where I pulled Red to a halt. Annie was still beyond my sight. The trail climbed into a heavily wooded slope which hid her from me but the muffled sound of hoofs told me she wasn't far ahead.

I was about to urge Red forward when the sharp bark of a rifle cracked the air. Then another. Red was in full stride seemingly without instruction from me. Another shot sounded as I swung around the road between high-branched trees. I could see the rig ahead, the horses spooked and running free. I couldn't see Annie.

A fourth shot kicked dirt from the ground a hundred yards in front of me. I stopped Red and looked up the slope to my right. There were too many trees for me to pinpoint the shooter's position by means of rising smoke, but the sound gave me the general area. I dropped the reins, took my saddle gun and slipped in among the trees, hoping that whoever was up there wasn't yet aware of my presence.

The next shot struck rock. I heard it ricochet followed by a squeal from Annie. Whether her reaction was from surprise or pain I couldn't tell.

Until that moment I hadn't been able to see her but now, her white blouse as plain to see as smoke signals against a blue sky, I spotted her curled and cowering near two small rocks. No doubt the angle from which I could see her gave me a clearer view than that which her attacker had, but she couldn't lie in such a cramped position for long. Wherever the gunman was he apparently had a clear shot if Annie showed herself. Ideally, I wanted to circle round behind the man and get the drop on him from above, but now, knowing how precarious Annie's position was, I had to prevent him shooting at her again. I figured if he knew I was around he would hightail it out of the wood.

Off to Annie's right, less than ten yards from her, a fallen pine offered more cover. It was long and high, and, once behind that, the shooter would have to make his way down to the trail if he wanted to finish off the job. But there was no way Annie could reach it without me diverting the gunman's attention. Nor did I know if Annie was able to make a dash for the tree. Perhaps she'd been hit. She certainly lay very still.

I retraced my steps back to Red and went behind him, removing my hat and hanging it on the saddle horn as I did so. I was on Annie's side of the trail; with luck I wouldn't have to reveal myself before I could assess her situation. Hopefully I'd be able to give covering fire while she made a dash for the greater security of the fallen pine. If the gunman fired again before I reached Annie then I would have to return fire wherever I was.

There was less cover on this side of the trail but the land did slope away so I kept as low as possible, confident that my dirty buckskin was good camouflage against the landscape. I covered the first forty or fifty yards at a crouched run, hoping that my head remained below the level of the trail. From there, where the trail straightened out and ran past the rocks where Annie lay, the slope became less pronounced and I was forced to crawl and snake my way towards her. No shots came from the hillside, aimed neither at me nor at Annie. I began to wonder whether I had got here too late. Whether the last shot had killed Annie and the gunman had fled.

I chanced a look across the trail. I could see why that spot had been chosen for the ambush. There was no gentle, wooded slope at this point, just a jagged hillside, like a cake with a huge mouthful removed. No doubt there were ledges and boulders enough to provide a commanding view of the trail below. I looked for some sort of movement up there but nothing presented itself. I put my head down and crawled on.

The situation changed when I was ten yards from her cover. I could see that she was almost curled around a third boulder which was behind the two I had been able to see earlier. Her feet were nearest me and one of them moved, slowly, as though needing to be stretched but wary lest it become a target for the gunman.

'Annie,' I called across to her in as low a tone as possible.

I heard her gasp, surprised by the closeness of a voice, afraid I was the person trying to kill her.

'It's OK,' I said. It's Wes. Wes Gray. Are you hit?'

She began to turn her head, lifting it slightly so that her hat must have shown above the rocks. At the same time I heard a rush of tumbling stones and rubble from the hillside. He was moving, coming down to the trail to finish off Annie. Then he shot, the bullet again striking rock, causing Annie to flatten her cheek against the ground.

I got to one knee and answered with three quick shots. Judging by the direction the shot had come from he hadn't come down the open face of the hillside but had circled round to use the cover of the trees on the slope to our right. I had the satisfaction of hearing him diving through bushes to escape my bullets.

'Annie,' I called, this time the need for secrecy removed.

'Yes?'

'Can you move?'

'Yes.'

'When I open fire again I want you to make for that fallen tree. Get behind it and wait until I come for you. OK?'

'Yes.'

'Ready?'

'Yes.'

I raised my head. Everything was quiet. I scanned the slope hoping to catch a movement, a glint from a gun barrel, the scrape of a boot upon rock. I needed to know his whereabouts. Did he intend to finish what he had started? Was he still coming towards us, or had my presence changed his mind? I fired a shot at the same place that I'd fired the other three. There was no response, but further up the slope I sensed a movement through the trees, a shape, a shadow, nothing more. 'Go,' I yelled at Annie. As she made a dash for fresh cover I stood and fired at the movement I'd seen, then followed behind but leapt the fallen tree and made for the hillside across the trail. As I passed her I dropped my handgun at her feet. She'd proved yesterday that she knew how to handle guns, if things went wrong for me on the hillside she now had the means to protect herself.

I set off up the hill, darting from tree to tree, carefully, though pretty sure there was too much wood between us for him to get any sort of a clear shot at me. It didn't take an Indian tracker to identify the bush he'd dived into when I'd snapped off those rapid shots at him. He'd gone in clumsily and heavily. Round about I could see broken stems and twigs, and here and there, boot imprints, showing the route he'd taken back up the slope.

I also found the spot where he'd fired his last shot at us. The ejected shell case lay near a heavy boot-print. I picked it up and looked for the scratch that had distinguished those that Hawk had found on the ridge above the Darke ranch house. It was there. I put the empty case into a spare loop on my gunbelt.

I followed the tracks, a bit more wary now. If he knew I was trailing him he could have found some advantageous position to wait for me. Whoever he was, he favoured bushwhacking when it came to removing opponents. I was three-quarters of the way to the summit when the first shot came, splintering twigs and scraps of bark from the tree I was passing. I stepped back behind it and waited for the flash of another shot before replying with two of my own.

After some seconds of inactivity I drew another shot by risking a look around the tree. The bullet whined away down the hill but not before sheering off a splinter that dug into my face just inches from my left eye. I pulled it out and used a kerchief to dab at the blood that flowed down my cheek. He had me pinned down. Going forward wasn't an option. To my left was the open hillside that offered no cover and no advantage to me. I needed to get deeper among the trees to my right, but even then there were stretches sparse of cover. Crossing them would make me a clear target. However, if I succeeded I would be able to circle behind him and the advantage would be mine.

I lay on the ground and wormed backwards in such a manner that a tree always obstructed the gunman's view. An elderberry bush was my first target and from there I moved further downhill but off to the right, taking me further away from the shooter. It had been several minutes since we'd exchanged shots and I knew my adversary would be becoming suspicious. I stayed on my belly and began the long crawl round the trees and back uphill until I came to the first of the clearer stretches I had to cross. The grass was lush here and quite long. I'd crept up on buffalo in shorter grass than this. To prevent the possibility of sunlight striking the barrel of my rifle I kept it tight against my right side as I squirmed slowly through the grass. I paused every so often, checking the direction I was taking and throwing looks towards the spot I'd last known the would-be killer to be. On one occasion I caught a movement, saw a branch moved by a rifle and figured that if I moved quickly I could draw a bead and hit whoever held it. But it was too risky. If I hit him but only winged him he would see me out in the open and would have a clear shot at me; alternatively I might shoot and kill him, which wasn't what I wanted either. There were questions to be asked. For the moment I wanted this man alive. I moved on.

When I reached the edge of the second clearing I paused and assessed my position. I couldn't cross the clearing in less than six strides, a long time to be in the open with a marksman waiting to kill you, but beyond lay the high ground I sought. The ground-cover here was more sparse than had been available at the earlier clearing, nothing more than a thin carpet of moss clinging to the rocky surface, minimizing the appeal of trying to cross with stealth. Still, whichever way I chose to reach the higher tree-cover, bold or cautious, was a gamble with odds only in my favour if the ambusher thought he still had me pinned down behind the tree further down the hill.

I chose bold. I broke from cover and ran in a crouch across the clearing. A bullet whistled over my shoulder before I'd completed my second step. Perhaps he'd seen me before I began the run, if not, his reactions were as sharp as a war tomahawk. I dived forward and rolled and rolled and rolled, almost colliding with the tree I'd mentally marked as my safety target. Two more shots were fired, each bullet striking rock that I had barely left behind, but now I had the high ground and good tree-cover, and I could go after my man.

He knew that, too. Foresaking his ambush position he began moving away through the vegetation. I could hear the rustling of leaves and branches ahead of me and, occasionally, the sound of boot on rock as he scuffed his way up the slope. He wasn't trying to disguise his flight so it occurred to me that perhaps his horse was close at hand.

Rather than blindly follow him I set course for the top of the hill, hoping to intercept him where the trees were more sparse. I ran along the ridge, straining to hear some tell-tale sound that would give away his location. I was sure he was still somewhere among the trees below me but I could no longer hear his progress through the undergrowth. I stopped, lay flat and put my ear to the ground. It gained me nothing. Then I heard it, the cry of a surprised horse some short distance ahead through the trees. Then there was a man's voice, urging the horse to an immediate gallop and hoofbeats heading my way. I ran on, my rifle in my hand ready for use.

They were below me, man and horse, following a trail on the far side of the hill. I couldn't see his face, his back was all but to me and he was bent forward over the horse's neck, huddled, like an Indian in his blanket when the snows have come. He was wearing a black hat and a brown jacket and still carried his rifle in his hand. The horse was nothing more than a rangy, dull brown cow pony, but its trappings made it unique. The saddle was of the Mexican style, a high cantle with silver workings in the bridle and breast-belt, and down the leg-leathers for the stirrups. I fired a shot after them. Not in the expectation of hitting anything, just to let him know I'd seen him and to make a promise that we'd meet again.

CHAPTER TEN

It seemed the sensible thing to do to make plenty of noise when I came back down the hill and called Annie's name before I got within revolver range. I also whistled for Red who skipped along the trail like a rodeo pony about to do tricks.

Annie showed herself with, I thought, a degree of apprehension, and I noted that she kept the revolver cocked until she was sure who was coming across the trail towards her. She began to smack the dust from her jeans and blouse, and brushed her hair roughly with her hands to get it into some sort of order. Part-way through asking if I got the gunman she noticed the blood on my face. She poured some water from the canteen on my saddle on to her own neckerchief and bathed my cheek. Meanwhile I told her that her assailant had got away but looked to be heading into town.

'Yes,' she said, 'that trail joins with this one about a mile from Beecher's Gulch.'

Tending my face wound took her mind off the

attack but when she got behind me and she wrapped her arms around my waist I could feel tiny tremors of shock passing through her. She rested her cheek against my shoulder. 'Who's doing this,' she asked, her voice so hushed I wasn't sure if it was meant for me to hear. 'Why is someone trying to kill me?'

'I'm not sure,' I said, 'but we're going to find out.'

We came across the buggy a mile or so down the road, the horses standing in shade chewing on the leaves of a purple-flowered shrub. I handed Annie up on to the long couch seat, tied Red to the rear, then got in beside her and took the reins. My rifle slotted nicely between us, butt down on the floor, barrel resting against the seat. I didn't hurry the horses, Annie needed some time to compose herself before we hit town. Still, there were questions to be asked and this was a good opportunity to ask them. Perhaps between us we could figure out what this business was all about.

'Seems it took people by surprise when you married Charlie Darke,' I said.

'Umm.'

'General expectation was that you would marry Chet Barton.' She looked at me as though she were about to tell me it was none of my business. I shrugged. 'Perhaps it's something to do with what's happening,' I explained.

'Don't see the connection,' she said. 'Chet

didn't get Charlie arrested and Charlie didn't shoot Chet.'

'None the less,' I said, 'I'd be interested to know why you changed your mind.'

Perhaps I was digging too deep into personal stuff, but she'd come to me during the night needing someone to talk to: I didn't think I was taking the conversation much further. She was quiet for a moment or two, then told me the full story.

'Duke Barton has been in this valley longer than anyone else. His folks settled here when he was younger than I am now. He married a girl from Ohio, the daughter of his father's friend. She hadn't seen Duke for ten years when she came out here. They were just children when they'd last seen each other. Didn't know if she'd still like him or he her. But she came and they married and raised two sons before a fever took her off. And Duke and she were as happy as any of the other couples who came to Beecher's Gulch.' She tucked a wisp of hair under her hat, a gesture, I thought, to give her time to put her thoughts in order. 'As you know, the Bartons have the biggest range hereabouts. Frontier people are jealous of their property, careful about straying over boundary lines. When you're one of the smaller ranchers you're always aware of the power that the bigger rancher wields. If he wants your land he brings his own law to bear to get it. It had happened to my father in another county. I'm not saying that Duke Barton

106

ever tried to cheat my father. They were good neighbours, even friends to a certain degree, but my father was always cautious when it came to trusting Duke Barton. So, when Chet and I started seeing each other, Pa wondered if Duke would allow his son to marry me. "Probably want some girl from the East for him. Someone brought up a lady, not a local ranch girl." I know he was thinking about Duke's wife coming special from Ohio but Chet had never suggested that that would be the way with him.'

I knew Annie's pa had been mistaken. Duke himself had told me that he'd expected Annie to marry his son.

'Then, a few months ago,' she continued, 'Chet and Duke went East without any explanation. They were gone some time and I heard nothing from Chet. Charlie Darke hadn't long been in town and he and Pa seemed to hit it off straight away. And he was nice. To me. You know what I mean?' I smiled and nodded, heck, it wouldn't be difficult to be nice to Annie. 'Then he got into that trouble with the foreman from the Silver Star. Killed him. Pa brought him out to the ranch to work. One night, setting on the porch after dinner, Pa started wondering about Duke Barton. What had taken him East and kept him from his ranch so long. Charlie said he'd overheard Wade Barton telling folks that they'd gone to find a wife for Chet. Some family friend. Same as Duke's pa had done for him.' Annie breathed deeply, holding on to her emotions.

'And you believed Charlie?'

'Why wouldn't I? Pa had suspected something like that.'

'And you?'

Her voice went small. 'I was surprised. Hurt, to be truthful. But Charlie had no reason to lie, and if that was what Wade was telling people it left little room for doubt.'

'But Chet didn't come back married.'

'No. But by then Ma and Pa had had their accident. I was alone. Wade Barton came by with an offer for the ranch but I said I wasn't selling. There were one or two hands around the place who'd been with us some time, men I could rely on, but I needed something more than that. Charlie proposed. I liked him and it seemed that Chet wasn't meant for me. That's how it happened.'

'I think both your pa and Wade Barton were wrong. Duke would have been proud to have had you married to his son.'

'Perhaps not now,' she said.

'You've got to sort out things with Charlie before you can think of anything else,' I said.

By now we were approaching town. It was still early, I could see a couple of youngsters scuttling along, wrestling as they went, towards a small whitewashed building that had every appearance of being a schoolhouse. Along the street I could

see the slim man from the store once again brushing his sidewalk. I had intended making my first
call at the livery stable to see if there was a recently
galloped horse there, but it wasn't necessary. I saw
it tethered outside the hotel, where the doors were
open for breakfast.

I stopped the buggy and got off, took my rifle
and slipped it into the saddle boot before untying
Red. 'Go along to the sheriff's office,' I told Annie.
'Tell him what happened on the way here. I think,
perhaps, I've found our man.'

'Be careful, Wes,' she said.

I tied Red next to the dull brown cow-pony with
the Mexican saddle. I wiped my hand across its
flank. It was hot and dusty from a long gallop. The
storekeeper was watching me. I walked to the door
of the hotel and looked in. A man in a brown coat
and black hat leant against the bar. I knew him. It
was the big man who had slapped the horse when
they'd tried to hang Charlie Darke and who'd
been anxious to see me and Charlie hanged for
the shooting of Chet Barton. He turned his head,
saw me, then threw back the shot of whiskey that
was in his glass.

I turned away and went across the street. The
storekeeper, who had resumed brushing the
boardwalk, put up his broom as I approached him.

'You look like a man who'd be a prominent
member of the citizen's committee,' I said.

He nodded. 'Theo Dawlish' He looked up at the

paintwork on his shop front where his name was displayed in large, black letters. 'What can I do for you?'

I removed the spent case from my gunbelt and handed it to him. 'Examine that. Pay particular attention to that half-inch scratch.' He looked at it as directed then at me with a question in his eyes.

'Someone tried to kill Annie Darke on her way into town this morning. That shell was one of the bullets fired. Now,' I dug deep into the pocket of my buckskin jacket, 'I found these at the spot where the bushwhacker shot Chet Barton.' I dropped them in his hand.

'They've got the same mark,' he said.

'So been fired from the same gun?'

'I'd say so.'

'Well, keep those safe and come with me.'

Annie was approaching the sheriff's office as I turned to retrace my steps towards the hotel. Theo Dawlish propped his broom against the wall and followed. I pulled the rifle from the boot attached to the fancy saddle on the dull brown cow-pony, stepped away from the horses, pointed the rifle into the air and pulled the trigger. I ejected the shell and thrust the rifle back into the boot.

'Do you want to check that one?' I asked Theo Dawlish. He picked it up, turned it slowly in his long fingers then looked at me.

'The same,' he said. 'We'd better get the sheriff.' At that moment two things happened simultaneously. The big man stepped out of the hotel with a look that threatened violence, his right hand resting on the butt of his six-gun. Before anyone could speak a loud scream came from further down the street. It was Annie. Along with everyone else who had been drawn on to the street by the shot I'd fired in the air, my head turned towards the sheriff's office where the scream had come from. Annie stumbled out into the street, eyes wide but seeing nothing other than whatever sight had caused her to scream. She cried again, an awful choking sound that couldn't find a proper release, then she collapsed in the street.

I was the first to reach Caleb's niece. She lay in the dust like a bundle of laundry, her face as white as death. I lifted her head but she had lost all consciousness. I looked up, pleased to see a matronlike woman bustling across the street. She knelt beside me and took over the task of reviving Annie.

When I got to my feet I saw Theo Dawlish in the doorway of the sheriff's office. He beckoned me, urgently, then disappeared inside. Satisfied that Annie was in good hands I followed Theo Dawlish. Sheriff Bayles was face down on the floor.

'Is he dead?'

'No. But he's taken quite a blow to the head. Gun-whipped, I suspect.' There a mass of congealed blood on the back of Dan Bayles's skull, and a fair amount of it in a pool below his head.

'Someone must have sprung Charlie Darke,' said the storekeeper.

'The sheriff kept him here overnight?'

'Hadn't been able to find the men who were Charlie's witnesses. Couldn't let him go until he did.'

The door that led to the cell block was open. There was no noise coming from there so I figured Theo Dawlish was right: someone had helped Charlie escape. I went through to be certain about that. The keys to the cells were attached to a big ring and were lying on the floor, as though discarded by someone in a hurry. There were three cells. All the doors were open but Charlie Darke was blocking the way into the middle one. His head hung to one side, his face was dark and his eyes and tongue were swollen. His body was stiff and unyielding; his feet several inches from the floor. The high frame of the iron-bar door had become a scaffold. Cruelly, he had been hoisted off his feet and left to choke to death, his feet, no doubt, desperately seeking the solidity of a floor which, to the end, he must have known was close at hand. There was no movement now. He hung there, ugly and disfigured. Whoever had been trying to kill Charlie Darke had now succeeded. The fact that he deserved to die prevented any feelings of remorse that I might have had for him, but, undoubtedly, Annie had found him like this, and I would have saved her that ordeal if I'd been able.

There were a number of men in the front office when I went back through. Dan Bayles was on a chair, the top half of his body slumped forward, the pain and dizziness too great for him to hold his head up. A short man with a moustache, busy eyes and a stern expression had taken charge, alternately firing questions at the sheriff and trying to organize a posse to catch Charlie Darke.

'Charlie Darke hasn't escaped,' I said. 'He's still through there.' I jerked my head towards the cells. 'Someone needs to cut him down.' That silenced the room. Even Dan Bayles turned his head in my direction though the action made him grimace with pain.

Two men went past me into the cell block. I heard one of them swear when he saw the body. 'Go get the undertaker,' I heard one of them say, and the other came back through the front office and hurried off down the boardwalk.

'What can you tell us, Dan?' the short man with the moustache asked the sheriff.

'Give him a few minutes, Lew,' said Theo Dawlish, 'he's taken a mighty blow. Somebody brew up some coffee and the rest of you get out of here. We'll let you know when we need you. For the present we've got to let Dan get himself pulled together.'

Although I wanted to be around when Dan Bayles began talking I accepted the sense in Theo

Dawlish's words. Also I was concerned about Annie. No matter how tough she was, the events of the morning were bound to have affected her.

'Do you know where they took Annie?' I asked Theo Dawlish.

'Try my store,' he said. 'I last saw her in the care of my wife.' He grabbed at my arm to prevent me leaving. 'What are we going to do about these?' He held the shell-cases in his hand.

'You can wait until the sheriff is able to arrest that big fella, or gather a posse of citizens together and do it now.' I opened the door to the street and paused. 'I'd like to hear what the sheriff has to say about the hanging of Charlie Darke. Perhaps we can get to the bottom of all the trouble that's been happening around here.'

CHAPTER ELEVEN

To the obvious distaste of Theo Dawlish's wife, Annie was unable to hold back a demonstration of her grief when I entered the back room of the store. She threw her arms about my neck and pressed a wet cheek against my chest. I could feel her entire body quake as great, gut-wrenching sobs escaped her mouth. She was unable to frame the questions she wanted me to answer, just clung to me as though I was the last refuge in a torrent. Not that I knew the answers; who had hanged her husband I couldn't say, why it had been done I could only guess at. Someone wanted Annie's land, at least they wanted the money the railroad were prepared to pay for the northern strip. I didn't tell her that, nor that Charlie Darke had deserved to hang for the murders of the Silver Star foreman and her parents. Someone would have to tell her one day, I hoped it wouldn't be me. I promised her I'd be around until the killers were caught. Mrs Dawlish, meanwhile, was trying to prise us apart like a sheriff with two barroom brawlers, and the scowl on her face told me that my behaviour was not that of a gentleman. None the less, I held Annie until the initial wave of her despair had passed, then led her to a sofa where I left her to recover until I was ready to return to the ranch.

For now I had more pressing business. The horse with the fancy Mexican saddle was no longer hitched in front of the hotel, which probably meant that the big man, too, had gone. I checked inside. A handful of men were gathered at the bar, disturbed from their work by the ruckus in the street and happy to discuss the matter with a glass in their hands before returning to their labour.

The desk clerk, a well-groomed man, looking cool despite the three-piece suit he wore, watched me as I paused in the open doorway. I crossed to him. He gave me a wary, professional smile.

'Yessir,' he said. 'Can I help you?'

'A few minutes ago there was a big man in here. Taking a drink at the bar.'

'Been a few men in here this morning,' he said. 'All the activity at the sheriff's office. Got people curious.'

'This man rides a Mexican saddle. Fancy silver-work embedded in the leather.'

'Sure,' he said. 'That would be Mr Grant. One of our guests.'

'A guest?' That seemed strange to me. He'd

been prominent in the earlier bids to hang Charlie Darke and if he wasn't a resident of Beecher's Gulch he had to have a reason for wanting Charlie dead. Only two offered themselves to me. Either Grant had trailed Charlie here seeking revenge for some previous wrong, or Grant had been brought here specifically to get Charlie. 'How long has Mr Grant been in town?'

'A few days. Let me see.' He ran his finger down the register book and stopped at an entry that only had three others below it. 'Cole Grant,' he said, 'from Virginia City. Came here Tuesday.'

I knew the name. Cole Grant was a hired gun. I hadn't run into him before but I'd spent enough time in Virginia City to know his reputation. He was a killer. It seemed probable that he'd been hired to kill Charlie and Annie Darke, and anyone else who got in the way.

'Do you know what business Mr Grant has here in Beecher's Gulch?'

'No sir. He didn't say.'

'Any idea where he might have gone?'

'Lit out of town riding east. That's the trail to Rapid City. Or,' he added as an afterthought, 'out to Duke Barton's spread.'

'The Silver Star?'

'That's right. Seen him drinking with some of Mr Barton's boys.'

I was confused. This information had brought me round in a full circle. When I'd arrived in

Beecher's Gulch the Silver Star outfit looked to be Annie and Charlie's likely persecutors. But the shooting of Chet and the talk I'd had with Duke Barton had convinced me otherwise. Now, if Cole Grant was in the pay of the Silver Star, a grab for more land and more power seemed a likely motive for the happenings hereabouts.

I left the hotel and went back to the sheriff's office. Apart from Theo Dawlish and the man called Lew who had assumed responsibility while the sheriff was incapacitated, another man, slight and elderly, hovered near the sheriff. The wound in Dan Bayle's scalp had been cleaned and covered with a sticking-plaster. I could tell by the glassy look in his eyes that there was still pain when he moved his head and his senses hadn't fully cleared. The newcomer kept glancing at Dan Bayle's face and letting small noises escape from his mouth as though surprised that the sheriff was still sitting upright.

'That's the best I can do for you,' he told Dan. 'I'll send someone for Tom Cartwright. He needs to take a look at you. That's a mighty whack you've taken. Yessir, a mighty whack.'

'You a doctor?' I asked.

'Nosir,' he said. I noted his quick speech, his habit of running his words together like the hotel clerk. Perhaps they were related, perhaps it was merely a local idiosyncrasy. 'The name's Harthope. Most of my customers usually have wings when I

118

get to them. I'm the undertaker. Still, in the absence of a proper doctor in town, I try to do what I can to patch up people 'til the doctor from Blackwater gets here.'

'He ain't coming,' I told him.

'What d'ya mean, ain't coming?'

'Doc Cartwright's dead.' When the shouts of disbelief ended I told the four men how Cartwright had been ambushed on his way to Annie Darke's ranch. 'I asked the riders who went for his body to have a look around for spent shells. My guess is,' I said to Theo Dawlish, 'that they'll match those that you're holding.'

'What's all this about?' Dan Bayles asked. I told him about the earlier attack on Annie and the experiment with the rifle from Cole Grant's saddle.

Theo Dawlish spoke. 'Reckon we need you to arrest him, Dan.'

'He's a hired gun,' I said. 'Better not tackle him on your own with that lump on your head. Besides, he's already skipped town.'

'Well he can't have got far,' said Theo. 'Let's get after him.'

'We'll get a posse together,' said Lew. 'Which way did he go?'

'It's only a guess,' I said, 'but I think we'll find him at the Silver Star ranch.'

'Duke Barton's spread!'

'The Silver Star seems to be involved in all of

Annie's troubles and Cole Grant has been drink-ing with Duke Barton's hired hands.'

'Duke wouldn't bring in a hired gun,' said Dan Bayles.

'Charlie Darke killed his top hand,' I said. 'Perhaps he thought he was too good with a gun to get rid of him any other way.'

'You've got Duke figured all wrong,' he said. Perhaps I had, and perhaps if Dan Bayles was in Duke Barton's pocket he was just trying to put me off the scent. There again, there had been nothing sham about the blow the sheriff had taken. It didn't seem likely he'd defend a man who'd been instrumental in cracking open his head.

'Come on, Theo,' said Lew, 'let's get a posse together and we'll ride out to the Barton spread.' When they left Harthope, the undertaker, went with them, assuring the sheriff that the body of Charlie Darke would be collected from the cells.

Dan Bayles was staring into the tin mug of coffee he held in his hand. I figured the news about Doc Cartwright wasn't what he wanted to hear. 'Ain't there a doctor in Beecher's Gulch?' He looked at me, confused by my question. 'Duke Barton told me about your blackouts,' I said. 'You'll be need-ing someone else to treat you.'

'Reckon so,' he said. 'Real neighbourly of Duke to discuss my problems with a stranger.'

'Just explaining why you hadn't been around to stop the attempt to lynch Charlie yesterday.'

'I don't need him or anyone else to defend my actions. Besides, he'll miss Doc Cartwright more than me. Don't suppose he told you about his own problems.' I shook my head. 'He's dying. Something growing inside him that's eating him away.'

'Cancer,' I said.

He nodded. 'Ain't got much longer. Don't suppose he'll see the start of another year.'

I remembered the man's scrawny neck, how my first impression had been of a man who'd lost a lot of weight. It also explained Hawk's decision to leave and his satisfaction at repaying his debt *before it was too late.* At the time I'd wondered at the meaning of his words, now it was apparent that he knew that Duke was dying. 'How long has he known?'

'Just a few weeks for certain. Took a trip back East a while ago. Him and Chet. Duke spent some time in a hospital but they had no cure for what ails him.'

'That the time their foreman was killed? And Annie's parents?'

'That's right. Weren't a pleasant homecoming for them.'

'I've heard it said that Chet went East to find a wife.'

'Hell no! It seemed pretty clear to most folks hereabouts that Chet would many Annie.' I was puzzled by Annie's sudden decision to marry

Charlie Darke, but, at times, grief makes people act strange. Dan Bayles was still talking. 'No, Duke needed a travelling-companion.'

'I suppose Wade was the better able to look after the ranch in his absence.'

The sheriff shook his head. 'I'm not saying Wade ain't a good cattleman, 'cos he is, but Chet is more like his old man. Thinks about things and puts the ranch first. Wade can be a bit on the wild side. Drinks and gambles and can't foresee any threat to the domination of the Barton family in this valley.'

'Can you?'

'Not while Duke's around.'

'After that?'

'I can't tell. I don't know what plans the brothers have for the Silver Star.'

'You think they might sell it?'

'They might split it. They're brothers. They don't always see eye to eye.'

I remembered the first time I'd seen Wade Barton. He'd thought his brother dead and his desire for revenge against the man he thought had killed him seemed genuine.

'Besides,' Dan Bayles said, 'I know that Wade has gambling debts. The Barton wealth is tied up in stock. I doubt if Chet will want to weaken the herd to help his brother out of a tight corner. His father won't.'

'The debt must be large.'

'More embarrassing than crippling. The eldest son of the biggest landowner doesn't earn any more than the hired hands. Wade's income doesn't satisfy his appetites.'

I let those words settle in my mind before asking the question I'd come for. 'Would you care to tell me what happened here last night?'

'Not much to tell.'

'Let's start with why Charlie was still in jail.'

'Clay Butler, who Charlie said he'd been with most of the day, had gone night-herding up on the far pastures. I told Charlie he had to stay in the cells until I'd spoken to Clay. I guess I let my guard slip. Didn't think lynching was on anyone's mind after Duke had vouched for Charlie.' Speaking the words brought home the realization that no one was likely to act against Duke Barton's wishes except Duke himself. He seemed to shake himself, dismissing the outlandish thought. 'It was late,' he went on, 'and there was a knock at the door and someone called for me. An urgent shout, but not loud, telling me a fight had broken out over at the hotel. I opened the door and looked out. Someone had their back to me, looking along the street to the hotel. I stepped out and that was the last I remembered. Someone hit me from behind. I knew nothing more until Theo and Lew were standing over me.'

'You didn't recognize the man? Or the voice?'

'Naw,' he said, but not in a convincing way.

'What is it?' I asked.

'Nothing. It was dark. I got hit pretty hard. I can't be sure that what I think I remember really happened.'

'Who do you think it was, Sheriff?'

'I didn't see his face. It was more an impression I got. The way he was standing, the size and shape of his body.'

'Who?'

'Wade Barton.'

'Wade!'

Dan Bayles protested again that his recollection of the figure outside his office was unclear. 'I ain't swearing that that was who I saw. Perhaps I'm wrong.'

A picture was forming in my mind, not a clear one, and here and there pieces were missing. 'What was Wade's reaction when the foreman was killed?' I asked.

'Straker! Wade acted responsibly. The Silver Star riders were all for stringing up Charlie Darke, but Wade told them to leave it to the law. I was obliged to him. I like to think that his father would have done the same thing but I was a bit surprised when Wade adopted that attitude.'

'Did his attitude change when you accepted it was self-defence?'

'Not really.'

'But it did change. When did that happen?'

Dan Bayles stroked his chin and looked thoughtful. 'Can't rightly say. They were friendly enough the day Annie and Charlie married.'

'He was at the wedding?'

'Sure. Duke and Chet were still out East but Wade was there.'

I recalled Annie telling me that it was Wade who had told Charlie that Chet had gone East to find a wife. No one else had suggested that, least of all Duke who was, according to Wade, the architect of the plan. But something had soured the relationship. Wade had arrived at Annie's ranch adamant that Charlie should hang for shooting his brother.

'Tell me about the railroad's offer to buy Annie's land.'

'They only want a strip on the northern range. Without it they'll be forced to lay tracks in the highlands, incurring huge costs for tunnel work and bridges.'

'Do you know how much they've offered for Annie's land?'

'Twenty-five thousand dollars. A good price.'

'But not good enough to tempt Annie or her parents before her.'

'It's good range with a stream that doesn't dry up in the hottest summer. That pasture keeps their ranch viable.'

'Supposing,' I said, 'that Annie had married Chet and the two ranches had united, how vital would it be to retain that strip of land?'

'Not vital at all. The Silver Star has plenty of

year-round water supplies. Annie's cattle could have been moved to any of the Barton's pastures.'

But Annie had wanted to maintain an independent ranch, and Chet had agreed with her. However, the lure of $25,000 was proving a temptation to someone. If that someone was Wade then it seemed he was prepared to stop at nothing, not even the death of his brother, to get it.

'I'm going out to the Silver Star,' I told Sheriff Bayles.

'Theo and Lew are gathering up a posse,' he replied.

'I can't wait for them. If Cole Grant is involved with anyone at that ranch I want to catch them before they can make plans to escape.'

'Who could he be involved with at the Silver Star? Not Duke.'

'No,' I agreed, 'not Duke.'

He regarded me for a moment. 'Wade?'

'I may be wrong,' I said, but there was little doubt in my mind.

He reached for his hat and tried to stand. 'Let me get my horse from the livery stable and I'll ride with you.'

'You're not up to it,' I said. 'I'd appreciate it if you got Annie back to her ranch. Duke Barton is still there. I'll meet you there as soon as I'm able.'

126

CHAPTER TWELVE

I guess I'd been on Barton land for some time when I came across the high, log-built gateway with a big metal star fixed in the apex. It wasn't made of silver but gave the same impression. A three-barred fence ran away to the distance either side of the gate and I slowed Red to a walk as I approached.

Two riders were exchanging words just the other side of the fence, but they cut short their conversation when they spotted me.

'Howdy,' I called. 'Is Wade at the ranch?'

'Yup.' One of the men nudged his horse forward to join me at the gate. He looked at me through tight-squinted eyes, squeezing out as much of the bright sun as he could. 'You the fella that dragged Chet into Charlie Darke's ranch house?'

The questioner spoke in a flat voice, giving no clue to his motive for asking. It seemed probable that there were divided loyalties among the ranch hands, some of them taking their orders from Wade. If that were the case, and they were putting their guns to his cause, I probably had to come up against them sooner or later. Better to meet them like this, one or two at a time, rather than find myself against an armed group. My right hand rested on my thigh, close to my six-gun when I nodded my head.

'You done a good thing. Don't have much liking for your friend, Charlie Darke, but I hear tell you done a brave thing in staying with Chet. Will he live?'

'With proper care he should make it.'

He reached over his horse's neck to undo the gate for me. 'Just follow the road,' he said. 'Ranch house is best part of a mile ahead.'

'Anyone else ridden through here recently?'

'Ain't seen anyone. How about you, Chuck?'

'Saw someone about ten minutes ago. I was fixing the fence up there.' The other man pointed to the rising ground off to his left.

'Did you recognize him?'

He removed his hat and wiped a line of sweat from his brow with his sleeve. 'Didn't take a lot of notice. Weren't one of our men.'

'Could it have been Cole Grant?'

He repeated the name trying to figure where he'd heard it before.

'Big fella,' I told him. 'Stranger in town. Rides a fancy Mexican saddle.'

He thought a moment. 'Yeah. Yeah. Could have been him. Sure could have been him.'

'I'm obliged to you.' I touched my hat and turned Red toward the ranch house.

The house nestled in a crescent-shaped canyon, the trail to its front door following the ridge of the descending hills from the rear, around the right-hand side to the valley floor. I reined in Red and took in the house and surrounding buildings. A couple of horses were tied to the rail in the yard but I couldn't see any cowboys or other workers anywhere near the house.

Instead of following the trail round to the front of the house I guided Red down the steep incline to the rear corner. We came down slowly. I hoped those in the house wouldn't hear my approach. Red is as sure-footed as a mountain cat and made light of the descent. I stepped down, dropped the reins in front of him and walked quietly to the house.

The side window gave me a view of the kitchen. It was empty. The door near at hand led into it so I used it. I could hear voices somewhere deeper in the house. I drew my gun and tried to find them. The bulk of Cole Grant filled a door-way that led off the main living-room. He had his back to me but I sensed an air of impatience in his stance. His right hand grasped the door-frame while his left shoulder pressed hard against the opposite side. One leg was bent and his head was bowed, his gaze fixed to the floor in front of him.

Wade Barton's voice came to me from within the room. 'You'll get your money when you finish the job.'

'I finished it. Last night. One thousand dollars to get rid of Charlie Darke. He's dead and ain't coming back.'

'A thousand dollars! I don't think so. I had to do half the job myself.'

'Wouldn't have been necessary if you'd just let me shoot him. I could have called him out and killed him the first day I got here.'

'Perhaps he was faster than you,' Wade Barton's tone was contemptuous.

Grant's deep throated chuckle was scornful of the attempt to rile him. 'I know Straker was your top hand, but he was still just a cowboy. Killing him didn't mean that Darke was a special sort of gunman. He may have double-crossed you, Wade, but I could have taken him whenever I chose to.'

'Even so,' a more subdued Barton responded, 'there's more required than the death of Charlie Darke. I want that ranch, and soon. Perhaps Annie will sell it to me now that her husband is dead.'

'If that Indian-lover hadn't turned up this morning she'd be out of the way, too. As it is I think he suspects that I attacked her. Could be he's got a posse after me already. It's not safe for me to hang around here any longer. Give me my money and I'll be out of here. You'd have some explaining to do if they found me here with you.'

'If you want a thousand dollars you've got another task to do first. You haven't lived up to your reputation, Grant. Your shooting ain't that hot. My brother. He's going to live. Get over to Darke's ranch and finish him off. Annie'll have no reason to stay here after that. Then when my pa's time comes I'll have both ranges and control of most things hereabouts.'

'OK if I just shoot your brother?' Grant's voice was loaded with sarcasm.

'I don't care how you do it. Just get it done.'

'Then give me my money. I'll finish him before I leave the territory but I gotta get going now.'

'It's too late,' I said. He swivelled on his left leg, his right hand grabbed the butt of his pistol, but when he saw that mine was in my hand and pointing at his middle he moved no more. 'Come away from that door,' I told him, 'and carefully take your gun from your holster and lay it on the floor.' When he'd done that I got him to kick it towards me. 'Now you, Wade,' I called. 'Better make sure I see your empty hands come through that doorway first' After ten seconds without any response I spoke again. 'Grant's right. There's a posse on the way. They can't be far behind. You can't escape.'

131

I heard the creak of timber, a floorboard being relieved of weight, and the light scrape of a boot across the floor. Wade was close against the dividing wall, wavering as to whether to come out fighting or not. Grant's eyes slid in his direction, then back to me, advising his partner of my position. I fired two shots at the door-frame, splintering the wood at head-height, forcing Wade either to throw out his gun or come out firing. A man whose caution has lasted as long as Wade's usually needs a mighty swing of fortune in his favour before he comes out fighting. Knowing that I was armed and prepared to use my gun tipped the balance my way. Wade threw out his gun and came out with his hands in the air.

There was a long, low couch in the middle of the room. I motioned for them to sit on that at each end. It would be difficult for them to launch an attack at me from a low, sitting position.

'There's nothing much lower than a man who pays to have another killed,' I said to Wade. 'Especially when the man is your brother.'

Neither of my prisoners spoke.

'Do you want to tell me the whole story while we wait for the posse?'

Again no one answered.

'So Charlie Darke double-crossed you, Wade. What was he supposed to do? Marry Annie then sell her spread to you?'

'No one would have been hurt if he'd done what

we agreed.'

'No one? What about Annie's parents? She never would have married him if he hadn't killed them.'

He threw me a dark, dangerous look, unsure how I knew that Charlie had murdered Joe and Louisa Brookes.

'Nor would she have married him if he hadn't told her that Chet had gone East in search of a society wife. That was your idea, wasn't it!'

Again, the only reply was a surly look.

'What kind of man are you? You didn't even want Annie's ranch, did you? Just the railroad's cash for that northern strip. So what happened? Did Charlie want more?'

'More!' Angrily Wade tried to stand up, but I motioned with my handgun for him to stay seated. 'What more could he want. He married the girl and had her ranch to sell. But he wouldn't do it.'

It was my turn to be perplexed. 'Why not?'

'Who knows. Conscience. Love. Claimed he couldn't deceive her. She wanted to keep the land intact and he agreed with her.'

'So you had to get rid of him by bringing in Grant and the gunnies I shot last night. I don't understand why you didn't pick a fight with him, why you went to all the bother of trying to frame him as a cattle-thief.'

'If he was lynched I couldn't see Annie staying around Beecher's Gulch The disgrace of being the

133

wife of a rustler would drive her out.'

It occurred to me that Chet Barton might have taken an interest in whether Annie went or stayed, and at the same time realized that Wade had had the same thought; that was why he had bought his brother's death, too.

'And Doc Cartwright,' I said, 'you had him killed knowing it would also foreshorten your father's life. How many lives had you planned to take to pay off some gambling debts?'

'My father's life is finished. What difference does a few weeks make. Soon,' he said, 'I'll control all the valley. And to celebrate I'll just take a glass of that whiskey.' He began to stand.

'Don't,' I told him. 'And they don't allow celebrations in jail.'

His sudden cockiness flashed a warning in my mind, and in my back I felt the prod of a gun barrel.

'I was in the stables, Wade. Saw him sneaking down from the trail.' The man reached around me and took my gun from my hand. I should have known that Wade and Cole Grant weren't alone at the ranch. The spread was too big for there not to be chores done about the place, and this old man, despite saying he'd been in the stable, had kitchen aromas, bacon, flapjacks and coffee, lifting from his clothes with every movement. He was a grizzled fellow, the sort who had been the butt of a thousand mealtime jokes, but there was nothing funny about the way his gun was bruising my back.

'Well done, Roly. Where's my gun.' Wade came across the room to collect his weapon. As he drew alongside me he released all his anger and fear in a blow to my jaw. I sprawled on the floor and in an instant Cole Grant was above me delivering two ferocious kicks, one to my back and the other to my front.

I wrapped my arms around my upper body to prevent any more damage to my ribs; then, through the pain, I heard the sharp metallic sound of a gun being cocked. I turned my head and found myself looking into the long, black barrel of Cole Grant's Colt. His finger tightened on the trigger. I heard a harsh snigger and waited.

'Not here.' Wade Barton pulled Grant's arm aside. 'Take him out to the stable.'

Cole Grant pulled me roughly to my feet and pushed me towards the door. I saw the look on Roly's face, perplexed, worried by the fact that Grant was prepared to kill me in cold blood.

'That's the man who shot my brother,' Wade told him, giving a nod in the direction of me and Grant. 'Somebody's got to pay for it.' If Roly had any sort of argument to offer against my being killed out of hand, he wasn't given any opportunity to voice it. 'I'm riding over to the Darke ranch to see my brother,' Wade told Grant. 'Catch up with me when you've finished here.'

Pleased to have the upper hand, Grant pushed hard against my back and I stumbled off the front-porch step but didn't fall. He gloated at his superiority, relieved that the gun was no longer pointed at him.

'Got it all worked out and no one to tell it to. What a sad way to leave life.'

'It wasn't idle talk when I told you a posse was on its way. Doesn't matter what you do to me, you can't get away with what you've done.'

'How will they know what I've done without you around to speak up?'

'I've already given them proof. They know that the bullets that were fired at Annie Darke this morning and those fired at Chet and me yesterday came from the same gun. And probably by now they know that the bullet that killed Doc Cartwright also came from that gun.'

'And what does that prove?'

'It proves that whoever owns the gun that fired those shots is the killer.'

'So?' He tried to sound confident but worry dripped from the single word.

'So this morning I proved, and had witnessed, that the gun is yours. They'll hunt you down, Grant. You'll hang for the murder of Doc Cartwright no matter what else you're guilty of.'

'Shuddup,' he said, 'and keep walking.'

Behind us I heard the ranch-house door open

and close. I sensed Cole Grant turn to see what was happening but didn't rate very highly my chances of turning and overpowering him before he could pull the trigger of the gun he was holding at my back.

I heard the creak of leather as someone, Wade I supposed, climbed into a saddle, then the steady drum of hoofbeats as horse and rider headed away from the house.

'Well, he's gone,' I said, 'and still hasn't paid you.'

'What!'

'Wade. Ridden off but I don't remember him putting any money in your hand.' There was a silence that could only mean he was pondering over my words. 'I was thinking,' I continued, 'that he seemed prepared to give his last partner a lot more than he's giving you. A ranch and a woman. Worth a lot more than the thousand dollars he hasn't paid you.'

'Shuddup!' I felt the iron of his gun thrust into my back.

We had turned the corner from the front of the building and were heading down the side towards the outbuildings.

'Do you suppose you'll be able to do this job on your own?' I was talking for the sake of it. Hoping I could find some way to distract him long enough to give myself a chance to overpower him.

'What do you mean?'

'You needed Wade's help last night when you hanged Charlie Darke.'

He laughed, but it was without mirth. 'Wade knocked on the sheriff's door. That's all Wade did. Don't worry, Indian man, I won't need any help to kill you.'

CHAPTER THIRTEEN

Cole Grant jabbed the barrel of his gun hard into my back. 'Keep going,' he said. 'Round the back of the barn. No need to scare the horses in the stable.' He gave one of his coarse, mirthless laughs. I half-turned my head. 'Keep going,' he said. 'Don't get any ideas. I don't mind shooting you here.'

But I did have an idea. We were passing close to Red who stood patiently in the spot where I'd left him. He lifted his head and studied us as we began to pass behind him. I made a clicking sound with my tongue and saw his ears prick up.

Grant poked the gun at me again. 'What you doing?'

'Nothing,' I said, but by now I had passed behind Red and gave a sharp whistle. I rolled to the ground and simultaneously heard a yelp of pain from Grant and a gunshot. Red had kicked out, his rear hoofs hitting Grant with sufficient impact to lift him off his feet and drop him in the dust some five yards from me. He'd hung on to his gun, but, dazed by the unexpected blow, his reactions weren't quick enough to bring it into play.

I gained my feet in an instant, ran forward and kicked the Colt from his hand. I grabbed a handful of his shirt and attempted to haul him to his feet. Cole Grant was a big man, and strong. He'd shaken off his surprise and brought his right fist up from the ground to punch me on the side of the head. I stumbled backwards, almost falling, but eventually keeping my balance. Grant had begun to slither towards his gun. I took a couple of steps and jumped on his back, bending my knees as I landed to drive the breath from him.

Astride his back I tried to get a grip around his throat but, besides his strength, it was clear that Cole Grant was no stranger to rough-house fighting. He grasped a handful of dirt and threw it over his shoulder into my face. My eyes stung as the dust covered them and, temporarily, I released my hold on him while I tried to clear my vision. He heaved me off his back and threw another right punch. I saw the blow coming only with enough time to turn my head so that it caught me behind my left ear. It carried enough force to pitch me face down into the dust. Now Grant was on my back, his hands locked on my forehead, pulling backwards, his knee pressed against my spine. I jabbed back with my elbow and felt his nose break. He cursed and, as spots of blood dropped into the dust, I rolled away from him. He was sitting on the ground, kicking his legs at me, hoping some lucky blow would incapacitate me.

Then he remembered the gun and turned his attention to finding it. It lay a couple of yards behind him. I saw it before he did, got to my feet and lunged at him before he spotted it. We wrestled for a few moments, each of us throwing punches with only a modicum of success. It wasn't possible for either of us fully to swing our arms or aim our blows as we grappled to gain the upper hand.

Then the fight turned in Grant's favour. We'd been struggling for supremacy, first one on top then the other, each trying to land a telling blow or get free for long enough to reach the pistol and put an end to the mêlée. We'd pushed each other away, got to our feet and somehow Grant came up with a length of timber in his hand, a broken carriage-shaft. It was over three feet long and in the hands of someone as powerful as Cole Grant it was a deadly weapon. It came at me in a great arc and crashed into my left upper arm. The blow lifted me off my feet. Once again I found myself with dust in my mouth, but that and the injured arm weren't my only discomfort. I had landed on something hard, something dug painfully into my midriff.

But now Grant stood over me, a gleam of victory in his eye. He lifted the great cudgel again, intent upon smearing my brains all over the yard. Before he could deliver the blow, Red came once more to my rescue, rearing above him, forehoofs clawing the air. Grant backed away from the assault with Red following him, snorting, stamping and rearing, until Grant turned and began running. I levered myself off the ground. Underneath me was Grant's gun. I picked it up and followed him and Red round to the front of the house.

Grant had reached his own horse and was slinging himself into the saddle. He pulled his rifle from the fancy saddle boot and jerked the mechanism to ensure a bullet was in the breech. He braced it against his hip and swung it back towards the corner where I stood. But this time I wasn't his intended target. It was Red he sought. Before he could aim I fired the Colt. The bullet didn't hit him but got close enough to make him reconsider his action. He fired at me. I felt the wind of the bullet pass my right ear. I fired again, the lead ricocheted off the corral rail. Urged on by Grant's spurs, the cow-pony leapt forward. Grant's rifle roared again, but, shooting backward from a galloping horse, there was little danger of being hit.

On the ranch-house porch stood Roly, the cowboy who had got the drop on me earlier. By his bemused expression I gathered he'd witnessed Red's pursuit of Cole Grant. He hadn't drawn his six-gun. I pointed the one I held at him.

'Take off that gunbelt and throw it over here,' I told him. He did so without speaking. 'Is that my gun you've got tucked in your waistband?' He touched the butt and lifted it clear. 'Gently,' I called. 'Throw that over here, too.' I picked it up, checked that the cylinders were loaded and put it in my holster. 'When the posse gets here tell them to get across to the Darke ranch as quickly as possible. Do you understand?' He nodded. 'Now lie down and stay down until I'm well clear of this place.' He did it in stages, down on one knee, then both knees, then pressed his palms flat on the ground before finally stretching his length on the porch. I climbed on to Red and slapped his neck. 'Come on, boy,' I said, 'let's finish this off.'

Grant's horse was kicking up dust more than half a mile ahead. He was hitting the ground hard, travelling fast, aiming, I suspected, to catch up to the slower-moving Wade Barton who was a further distance in front. Wade had started something he couldn't stop. What had begun as a way of getting his hands on some cash to pay off his gambling debts had snowballed. Now he would settle for nothing less than owning the Silver Star and Annie's Circle D ranch. He had proved he would stop at nothing to get them and now I suspected that the lives of his father, brother and Annie Darke were in imminent danger.

I didn't run Red flat out. What I'd seen of

Grant's pony, though a good working horse, didn't encourage the belief that it would be capable of maintaining its early pace for any great distance. Over a long run I had confidence in Red's abilities. I hadn't yet seen his match for speed and stamina. We followed at a steady pace, the land hereabouts being low and level so that I could see the pair in front. I'd covered more than a mile when they met up.

By this time they were approaching a more undulating landscape. I urged Red to lengthen his stride; this was strange territory to me and I had no wish to lose them. I galloped the mile that had separated us when Grant had reached Wade, certain that by doing so I had rapidly closed the gap between us, but, when I reached that point, they had disappeared into the folds of the hills. I slowed Red, constantly checking the ground for signs of their trail. It was clear enough to follow, the dry ground clearly showing hoof prints which I followed around the lower slope of one hill and over a rise into a dry valley.

I brought Red to a halt and scanned ahead, hoping to catch sight of them. Their mounts were still moving fast and their route followed the line of the valley. Half a mile ahead it curved away to the left. I was surprised that they were still so far ahead of me, but Wade had the advantage of knowing the terrain. There were no tell-tale wisps of dust to be seen, neither along the valley nor up the hillsides. I tapped Red's flanks with my heels and we continued the pursuit.

I hadn't covered a hundred yards before I spotted their ruse. I dismounted this time, taking my rifle from its scabbard as I did so. Knowing Grant's predilection for ambush it was to be expected that I'd be led into a trap. Probably it was Wade who chose the location but it had to be Cole Grant who was waiting to pull the trigger.

It was the hoof-prints that betrayed their plan. There had been a gradual slowing of pace, marked by the depth of print and shorter distance between strides, but then the pace had quickened again and the horses had run on to the bend in the valley. Now, however, one of the horses was lighter. The rider, probably Grant, had jumped off. It took only a few seconds to spot the disturbed scrub where he had landed, stumbled forward, then made a beeline for the slope which led to the crest of the hill.

Although I was well within rifle range from the hillside, no shot had been fired at me which could only mean that at that moment I wasn't under surveillance. There had to be a more advantageous position for a sniper further round the valley. I led Red into the shade of some cottonwoods then began a cautious climb up the hill, following the footsteps of my would-be assassin.

A light breeze blew along the crest of the hill, cooling my face and body as I pressed my ear to the ground. There were no vibrations. He'd found a good spot and now waited patiently for me to ride into his line of fire. I shuffled slowly forward, raising my head now and then, seeking a sound or a sight or a smell that would disclose his position.

Suddenly he was a mere handful of steps away from me, lodged between two boulders, one of which he was using as a rest for his rifle to give him extra accuracy. Despite the heat he hadn't removed his brown jacket, figuring, I guess, that his wait would be short.

I stood up and set myself in a firm stance. 'Grant,' I said, my voice soft and low allowing the breeze to take it to his ears. His shoulders stiffened, the grasp on his rifle tightened, his head turned ever so slightly as though satisfying himself that the wind hadn't lied. Then he spun, his rifle came up and his finger found the trigger.

But I fired first, the shot hitting him in the chest and pushing him further into the space between the rocks from where he'd hoped to shoot me. I fired again, then again. Each slug thumped into his chest, jerking his body deeper into the fissure. I left him there where death had claimed him, suspended, upright, the barrel of his rifle still gripped in his left hand.

From the top of the hill I looked into the valley below. Grant's pony, complete with fancy Mexican saddle, waited alone further along the trail. In the distance I could see the dust trail of Wade Barton's mount as it progressed on its journey north. If he'd heard the shots they didn't cause him to pause, but then, he wouldn't expect Cole Grant to make a mess of this ambush; his own liberty depended on it. But though he had failed it didn't alter the fact that he'd caused my delay. Ahead of Wade I recognized the hill line that formed the ridge above Annie's ranch. I had no hope of catching him before he got there.

I hurried down to Red, untied him, shoved the rifle into the saddle boot and swung myself into the saddle. He ran as he'd never run before, Grant's brown pony shying away from the trail, startled by the speed of our approach. Ten minutes later I was on the heights where Hawk had found the first spent Springfield shells. Without slackening pace I guided Red towards the road from town, then turned him to the fence line at Annie's ranch. As we came through the gate I snatched Red to an abrupt halt. Face down on the ground, the folds of her skirt lifting in the breeze, was a body. Even Red's speed had proved insufficient. I had arrived too late. I stepped down to take Annie in my arms.

CHAPTER FOURTEEN

There was an unexpected heaviness about the body when I turned it over, and a greyness about the hair that flipped in the breeze, and lines in the face that bespoke more years than Annie Darke had lived. My relief that the woman in my arms wasn't Annie didn't dissolve the block of anger in my guts. This woman, Mrs Lowe I presumed, who was guilty only of acting neighbourly, had died alone and in pain. Her hands were formed into two tight fists, her face distorted by the final agony. Blood had spread, ugly brown, over the bodice of her plain, grey frock. I laid her head on the ground and headed for the house.

There was an unnatural stillness about the place, an air of desolation such as I'd encountered at abandoned mountain cabins and worked-out mines. No birds sang, no sound carried, as it had the night before, from nearby herds or their human herders. The bunkhouse was silent as, too, was the ranch house. Even Wade's horse, loosely hitched to the veranda rail, stood motionless, head lowered, as though ignoring the death that had occurred in the yard.

It didn't seem possible that my arrival had passed unnoticed, but Wade expected Cole Grant to join him, perhaps he was so sure of his own schemes that he gave no thought to their being foiled. I drew my gun and cautiously peered through a window. There were signs of a scuffle. A chair was on its side and the table was displaced from its central position. A couple of cups were overturned on the table, and, on the floor near the door to the bedroom, lay Duke Barton. I lifted the latch on the door and stepped inside.

Sinister sounds came from the bedroom, sounds that were human but which didn't have their source in any physical experience. I couldn't describe them as growls or giggles, or groans or moans, but it seemed to me that they registered the culmination of some deep-seated need, though whether the person from whom they issued experienced joy or despair I couldn't tell. Stealthily, I crossed to the bedroom.

Duke Barton, grey and bruised, raised his head from the floor. 'Help,' he said, the word no more than a fading whisper.

'Help!' cynically repeated a voice from the bedroom, 'it's too late for that.'

I stepped over Duke and paused in the doorway. Wade looked at me over his right shoulder while pressing down on a pillow which covered Chet's face.

'That's enough,' I told him. 'Step away from the bed.'

I have observed three types of men under imminent threat of death: those who accept the inevitability of their fate and face it full on; those whose faith and bravery fails them and plead for the thin thread of their life to be sustained; and those who, by invention and trickery, seek to cheat Death's scythe. But which man will act in which manner is unknown to him unless that moment arrives. Wade Barton proved to be the resourceful kind.

How he picked up the lamp I cannot tell. One moment he had both hands pressed on the pillow then, at my command, he raised the pillow from his brother's head and turned towards me. Somehow, perhaps by screening his left hand with the pillow, he grasped the heavy lamp from the table by the bed and flung it at me. I fired, but it was a secondary reaction, my first being to fend off the object he'd thrown at me. Consequently my shot struck the roof. I took a step back, stumbled and fell over Duke Barton. Even so I was able to fire another shot before Wade could draw his own gun. That too was off target. Before I could fire again Wade slammed the door closed, leaving him in the bedroom and me on the floor of the main room. I fired a third shot but the door was too thick to be penetrated by a .45 slug.

'Come on out, Wade,' I shouted. 'The posse can't be far behind. You can't escape.'

I didn't get any response. I reloaded the three emptied chambers and threw a glance at Duke. His eyes were open and his lips were moving but if there was any sound coming from his mouth I couldn't hear it. His skin was the colour of uncooked dough and I knew he was dying. I couldn't see any bloody wound on his chest or head. I touched his hand with my own but could offer him no greater solace. My concern at the moment was for Chet who lay at his brother's mercy beyond the door. I had no immediate strategy to get either brother out of the room. Rushing the door would be suicide. I called again, and again Wade refused to answer.

The bedroom, I recalled, only had the one door, the one which connected it to the main room, but it did have a window. I figured that if I spoke to him again, convinced him that I was still in the front room, I could slip out through the door and get the drop on him from the rear window.

So that's what I did. 'Come on Wade, throw out your gun.' It was too late for that, of course. When he opened the door he would come out shooting. I spoke about the posse again, he would know that he had no chance of escape once they arrived. But all was quiet in the other room so I went outside, hurrying off the veranda and round the side of the house. I turned the corner at the same time as Wade came round from the back of the house. He'd come out through the window that I'd intended to cover him from. We saw each other at the same moment, and exchanged shots. He carried a rifle, a more dependable and accurate weapon than my six-shooter, so I dodged back around the corner, vaulted the veranda rail and squatted on the porch step. Suddenly Wade stepped into view, firing five or six shots that splintered wood from the veranda rails, wood from the chair by which I crouched, and lifted my hat from my head and sent it skimming through the air. I fired two quick shots, dived through the open doorway and kicked the door closed behind me.

Wade fired another fusillade, shattering the glass in the window where he expected me to appear. I kept my head down until it was over then risked a quick look. He saw me and fired again.

'Boot's on the other foot,' he shouted.

'What d'ya mean, Wade?'

'You're in there with the dead people. I'll tell the posse you killed them.'

'It won't work,' I called. 'They know I didn't have anything to do with killing Charlie Darke or trying to ambush Annie.'

'Perhaps so, but who are they going to believe killed my pa and brother? Me or you.'

'You think I have some reason to kill them?'

'You're a saddle tramp who spotted an opportunity. All you had to do was stop Chet marrying Annie then step in yourself. Land and railway money there for the taking.'

'Uh-uh, Wade. That doesn't work. I was sent here by Annie's uncle. Perhaps you didn't know that but other people do. Besides, there are people in town who know of your connection with Cole Grant. He was a killer. It won't take them long to tar you with the same brush. Besides which,' I shouted, 'your pa's still alive.'

There was silence for a moment, then, with a less certain voice, he called back, 'Guess I'll just have to come in and finish both of you off before the posse gets here.'

All the while the conversation had been going on I'd been busy. I'd gone to take Duke Barton's gun from its holster and found him dead. I rolled him half-way over and found the hole in his back that had done for him. There was a lot of blood on the floor under his body. I went back to the window and balanced his pistol against the frame with the barrel sticking out for Wade to see. I had just completed that task when Wade made his declaration of intent to 'come in to finish us off.'

At the same moment I saw dust rising from the town trail. There wasn't sufficient for it to be a hard-riding posse, but whoever it was, Wade hadn't yet seen them. I could see him down by the water-trough reloading his rifle, every now and then raising his eyes to the house to make sure I wasn't trying to make a break for it.

Then I recognized the rig that was approaching the ranch. It was Annie's. I couldn't let her ride into the gun battle without any warning. I fired a couple of shots at Wade Barton hoping she would have the sense to stop where she was until the fight was over. Wade fired back and I was showered with particles of glass and wood. I fired again, using Duke Barton's gun, then chanced another look up the trail.

To my dismay, rather than the rig pulling in for safety, it seemed as though the horses had been whipped to a greater speed. Annie was in dreadful danger if she got within Wade's rifle sights. I had to act immediately if I was to have any chance of saving her.

I fired towards the water-trough again and drew an answering two or three slugs. Then I dashed into the bedroom and out through the window, using the same escape route that Wade had used earlier. The water-trough was directly in front of the house so my journey from the back window, along the side to the front corner of the house, was undertaken unobserved. As I pressed myself against the rough timbers I could hear voices. It wasn't Annie demanding to know what the shooting was all about, it was a man. I recognised Dan Bayles's voice and recalled that I'd asked him to escort Annie home.

'Stop that shooting, Wade,' I heard him call, 'and put down your gun.'

'Can't do that, Dan,' Wade replied. 'There's a man in there just killed my pa and my brother.'

'Killed your pa?'

'That's right. And now I'm going to kill him.'

'That's a job for the law, Wade.'

I didn't catch Wade's answer but his gun began to swing up on Dan Bayles.

'Wade,' I shouted. He spun, expecting me to be in the doorway. I shot him, thrice. Each bullet staggering him backwards until he crumpled in a heap beside Annie's rig.

CHAPTER FIFTEEN

I remained in Beecher's Gulch for several weeks after the killing of Wade Barton. On the first night I was offered the hospitality of the sheriff's office, without the option of refusal. However, once Wade's connection with Cole Grant was established, and Roly, the Silver Star ranch hand, had told how Wade and Cole had planned, in cold blood, to kill me, my innocence, of which Dan Bayles had little doubt, was pretty well established. Added to that were the shells from Cole Grant's rifle at the scene of the attempted murders of Chet and Annie, and the actual murder of Doc Cartwright. Incidentally, when, following my directions, they recovered Cole's body, it was in such an advanced stage of *rigor mortis* that, in addition to the difficulty it presented them in extracting it from the crevice in which it was lodged, in a macabre twist of fate, his left hand was fastened tightly around the barrel of the rifle, as though even in death he could not deny its ownership.

I returned to Annie's ranch the next day and helped out around the place as best I was able. I didn't get involved with the cattle, she had drovers enough to handle that business and my appearance among the herds might well have been misinterpreted. I didn't want anyone thinking that I was trying to establish some superior position. To this end, to establish some sort of camaraderie, I bunked down with the cowboys at night. However, I took most of my meals with Annie. We liked each other, Annie and me, but, as I've said before, she was easy to like.

Chet survived. He stayed two days at Annie's after the death of his father, then he was transported home to be nursed back to health by an aunt, his mother's sister, who was sent for from Ohio. By coincidence, she arrived at Beecher's Gulch on the same stagecoach that brought Caleb Dodge to town. I had written to him, outlining the events that had left his niece a widow, and felt that, with a sizeable ranch to run, some family advice would be in order. Despite the discomfort of travelling with a leg that wouldn't bend and a crutch, Caleb had set out immediately to assist Annie, although, when he arrived, his first words to her somehow put a different slant on his prompt attention.

'Annie, m'dear,' he said, 'I'm sure sorry for your loss, but Wes here is married and we can't keep him from his wife too long.'

'Can't ever recall you saying that during six months on the trail to California.'

'Hummph!' he grunted.

Annie laughed. I'd told her about Marie, Sky and Little Feather and she'd accepted it. Perhaps, like her uncle, she harboured misgivings against the theory of a man having three wives, but she never formed any objection into words. In her own way, like me, she was a survivor. In this new land, survival wasn't just about getting food into your belly and finding protection against nature and disease, it needed a mental toughness that was equal to, if not greater than the physical durability. It was about moving on; reaching for a goal; knowing when to persevere with your principles and when to shake off those memories and events that hindered; and in those few days after Charlie Darke's death I knew Annie would be OK.

She'd cried when I told her about Charlie Darke, for that lot fell to me as I knew it would, but I never saw those tears again. She laughed sometimes and smiled a lot and her jaw set with determination in those quiet moments when I knew that thoughts of her future were being challenged by the losses in her past. I couldn't help her with that, that was a job for Caleb.

As it happened she never did many Chet Barton. Several years later I learned that the events of the summer of 1869 changed both of them, and an awkwardness in company with each other kept them apart. Chet married an Ohio girl, a family friend of the aunt who had come West to nurse him back to health, and Annie married Clayton Deane, MD, who replaced Doc Cartwright in Blackwater. She sold the ranch, northern strip and all, to Herman Lowe. The first thing he did was to plant a flower-garden on the spot where his wife had died. Before his death he became the largest landowner in the valley, buying much of the Silver Star range from Chet Barton who spent much of his time in the East.

Dan Bayles let it be known that he couldn't continue as a law officer, but he agreed to hold onto the job until a new sheriff could be appointed. A couple of days before I left Beecher's Gulch he called me into his office and handed me a slip of paper. It was a banker's order for $200 made payable to me.

'Cole Grant had a price on his head for the murder of two lawmen in Montana. You can redeem that for cash in any bank in the Union.'

Collecting money for killing a man who deserved nothing more didn't sit easy with me. I wasn't a bounty hunter and didn't want to get the sort of reputation with a gun that would make me a target for all the trigger-happy saddle tramps across the Plains. But then, I reasoned, I'd earned nothing that summer. Caleb Dodge had given my scouting job to someone else, and I'd come here, to Beecher's Gulch, with no other incentive than to do a favour for my friend.

I tucked away the slip of paper. Money in the pocket is a useful aid to survival; besides which, I have three wives to support.